"Maybe it's all your imagination,"
Jake said.

"I don't think so," Nog replied. "I ran all through the Promenade, and when I turned around, I could see that monster's eyes watching me, towering up above the crowd—"

Nog stopped short. With a trembling finger he pointed toward thin air. He yelped, "Look! Look there! It followed me!"

Jake stared in shocked disbelief. The living room lights had dimmed automatically at nine o'clock. Now, in the darkness, he could just make out a shimmering, transparent silver form, taller than his own father but so slim it looked emaciated. The face was in darkness, beneath what seemed to be a hood. The skin on the back of Jake's neck prickled into goose bumps. He could see nothing of the thing's features.

Except two glaring orange-red eyes.

Star Trek: The Next Generation

Starfleet Academy

#1 Worf's First Adventure
#2 Line of Fire
#3 Survival

Star Trek: Deep Space Nine

#1 The Star Ghost

Available from MINSTREL Books

THE STAR GHOST

BRAD STRICKLAND

Interior illustrations by
Todd Cameron Hamilton

PUBLISHED BY POCKET BOOKS

New York   London   Toronto   Sydney   Tokyo   Singapore

This book is a work of fiction. Names, characters, places and incidents are either products of the author's imagination or are used fictitiously. Any resemblance to actual events or locales or persons, living or dead, is entirely coincidental.

A MINSTREL PAPERBACK *ORIGINAL*

A Minstrel book published by
POCKET BOOKS, a division of Simon & Schuster Inc.
1230 Avenue of the Americas, New York, NY 10020.

This book is published by Pocket Books, a division of Simon & Schuster Inc., under exclusive license from Paramount Pictures.

ISBN: 0-671-87999-5

First Minstrel Books printing February 1994

10 9 8 7 6 5 4 3 2 1

A MINSTREL BOOK and colophon are registered trademarks of Simon & Schuster Inc.

Cover art by Alan Gutierrez

Printed in the U.S.A.

For Marilyn Teague:
"Hailing frequencies open!"

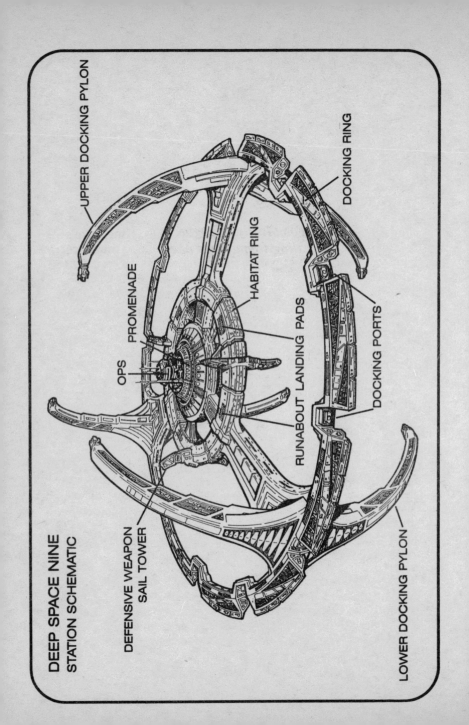

DEEP SPACE NINE
STATION SCHEMATIC

UPPER DOCKING PYLON

DOCKING RING

HABITAT RING

PROMENADE

DOCKING PORTS

OPS

RUNABOUT LANDING PADS

DEFENSIVE WEAPON
SAIL TOWER

LOWER DOCKING PYLON

STAR TREK®: DEEP SPACE NINE™
Cast of Characters

JAKE SISKO—Jake is a young teenager and the only human boy permanently on board Deep Space Nine. Jake's mother died when he was very young. He came to the space station with his father but found very few kids his own age. He doesn't remember life on Earth, but he loves baseball and candy bars, and he hates homework. His father doesn't approve of his friendship with Nog.

NOG—He is a Ferengi boy whose primary goal in life—like all Ferengi—is to make money. His father, Rom, is frequently away on business, which is fine with Nog. His uncle, Quark, keeps an eye on him. Nog thinks humans are odd with their notions of trust and favors and friendship. He doesn't always understand Jake, but since his father forbids him to hang out with the human boy, Nog and Jake are best friends. Nog loves to play tricks on people, but he tries to avoid Odo whenever possible.

COMMANDER BENJAMIN SISKO—Jake's father has been appointed by Starfleet Command to oversee the operations of the space station and act as a liaison between the Federation and Bajor. His wife was killed in a Borg attack, and he is raising Jake by himself. He is a very busy man who always tries to make time for his son.

ODO—The security officer was found by Bajoran scientists years ago, but Odo has no idea where he originally came from. He is a shape-shifter, and thus can assume any shape for a period of time. He normally maintains a vaguely human appearance but every sixteen hours he must revert to his natural liquid state. He has no patience for lawbreakers and less for Ferengi.

MAJOR KIRA NERYS—Kira was a freedom fighter in the Bajoran underground during the Cardassian occupation of Bajor. She now represents Bajoran interests aboard the station and is Sisko's first officer. Her temper is legendary.

LIEUTENANT JADZIA DAX—An old friend of Commander Sisko's, the science officer Dax is actually two joined entities known as the Trill. There is a separate consciousness—a symbiont—in the young female host's body. Sisko knew the symbiont Dax in a previous host, which was a "he."

DR. JULIAN BASHIR—Eager for adventure, Doctor Bashir graduated at the top of his class and requested a deep-space posting. His enthusiasm sometimes gets him into trouble.

MILES O'BRIEN—Formerly the Transporter Chief aboard the *U.S.S. Enterprise,* O'Brien is now Chief of Operations on Deep Space Nine.

KEIKO O'BRIEN—Keiko was a botanist on the *Enterprise,* but she moved to the station with her husband and her young daughter, Molly. Since there is little use for her botany skills on the station, she is the teacher for all of the permanent and traveling students.

QUARK—Nog's uncle and a Ferengi businessman by trade, Quark runs his own combination restaurant/casino/holosuite venue on the Promenade, the central meeting place for much of the activity on the station. Quark has his hand in every deal on board and usually manages to stay just one step ahead of the law—usually in the shape of Odo.

CHAPTER 1

There were times when Jake Sisko hated living on a space station. The fourteen-year-old Earth boy much preferred the open spaces and excitement of a living world to the metal and glass confines of Deep Space Nine. However, he had to admit that sometimes living here had its advantages. For one thing, it was easy to slip away from the adults and meet his friend Nog.

Nog's uncle Quark owned a bar and restaurant on the Promenade, the commercial section of the space station. Not too far away was the Bajoran-owned Galactic Adventures, a high-tech arcade where, for a price, you could play all sorts of holographic games. The arcade was a maze of booths, nooks, and alcoves, and it was just the place for a boy to meet his best friend—especially when the best friend's father disapproved of Earth boys.

With his school computer padd under his arm, Jake slipped into the darkness of the arcade and went past a booth where two visiting Bajoran kids were playing

Cardassian Shoot-out. The two were in a simulated Bajoran landfloater, and they were zipping through a battlefield of heavy Cardassian armored death-tanks, zapping tank after tank as they yelled with excitement.

Jake paused for a moment to watch. From outside the booth, the holographic effect was not as realistic as it was to the players inside, but it was still pretty convincing. He knew the two children were pretending to be Bajoran freedom fighters, hit-and-run daredevils who had struggled against the Cardassian overlords for years. Jake blinked as a death-tank exploded with a vivid flash and roar, and then he went on.

No one was playing the next game, Starfleet Commander, but someone was in a secluded corner just beyond playing Ferengi Trader. There Jake found Nog, listening intently to a computer readout being spoken in the hissing, whisper-soft Ferengi language.

"Hi," Jake said, sitting beside him.

The bald, huge-eared Ferengi boy barely glanced at him. "Just a moment," he said. "Let's see . . . if I hold on to my dilithium mines but sell my interest in the trans-system transport company, I could afford to—" He spoke some orders to the computer, and the readouts changed. After a moment a chime sounded, and the computer reported, "Congratulations, player. You have reached a new high score of fifty billion, three hundred and seventy million, one hundred fifty-seven thousand, nine hundred and seven. This qualifies you as a Ferengi Tycoon. If you wish to

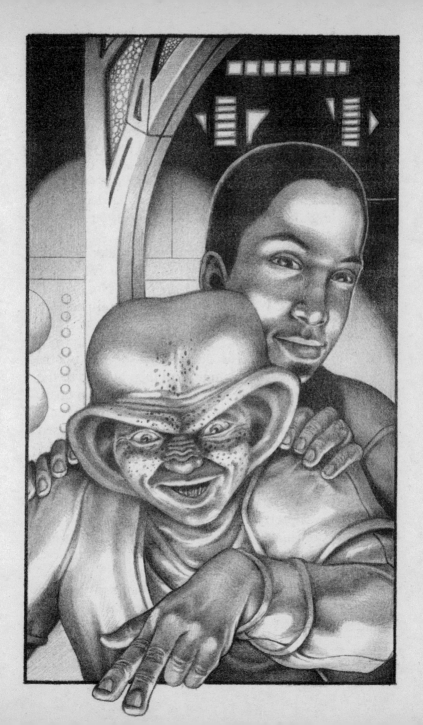

continue to play, transfer one credit within the next fifteen seconds."

"Too easy," Nog said, giving Jake a pointy-toothed grin. "I'll be a Plutarch by tomorrow, and I'll make Nagus by the day after. It isn't as much fun when it's not challenging—and you can cheat at harder games, too." He glanced past Jake. "You sure you weren't followed?"

Jake sighed. Ferengi were traders, wheeler-dealers, and con artists who valued profits above everything else. They were also very suspicious. "No, Nog, I wasn't followed. Where can we go that's a little more private?"

"That's taken care of," said Nog with a mysterious grin. "Follow me." He ducked out of the booth, glanced cautiously all around, and then hurried to the back of the arcade. An automatic door whished open, and Jake followed his friend into a small room, bare except for a round table and a few chairs. "This used to be the snack room," Nog explained. "That is, until my uncle tricked the owner into removing the food replicators. Now when players get hungry, they have to go next door to my uncle's place to eat."

"That was pretty smart of Quark," Jake said.

"Good business," replied Nog with another of his fierce grins. "Now, what's your problem?"

With a sigh Jake said, "It's still math."

Nog rolled his eyes. "What's the *matter* with you, Jake? Don't you see how important math is? And how much fun it is?"

"Fun!" Jake shook his head, put his school padd on the table, switched it on, and plugged in a data clip. "Algebra is about as much fun as—as stepping barefoot on a Klingon prickle-mouse! And when we first took up geometry in class, I remember you didn't like it yourself."

Nog looked sheepish. "Well, I'll admit that I used to find it hard before Uncle Quark explained things to me."

Jake blinked at Nog. Quark was a Ferengi with an overdeveloped greedy streak, a sly sense of humor, and a crabby attitude. Jake had never thought of him as a math wizard. "How did he explain algebra?" Jake asked.

"Oh, he didn't *explain* it. He just made it a lot more interesting," replied Nog.

"Okay, how did he do that?" asked Jake.

"Simple. Uncle Quark said that if we Ferengi know all the mathematics of all the life-forms in the galaxy, nobody can ever cheat us in a business deal. And besides, if we know some math that others don't—" Nog grinned, his sharp teeth wolfish.

"You can cheat them instead," Jake finished for his friend. He smiled. Ferengi values were not the same as those of humans. If a Ferengi passed up a chance of cheating someone, it was as terrible a mistake as it would have been for Jake to come to school wearing just his underwear. But Quark's pep talk on the advantages of math didn't help Jake. He sighed. "I think I could get it if only I could see how these numbers go together. Anyway, I wondered if you would just help me with this homework."

"Your dad can't help you?" asked Nog.

Jake made a face. "I don't want to ask him," he said. "He's too busy." Jake's father, Starfleet Commander Benjamin Sisko, was in charge of Deep Space Nine. He had to keep peace among the dozens of different intelligent species on the station, guard the Bajoran Wormhole that led to the far side of the galaxy, and do a hundred other jobs.

Right now, for example, he had to play host to a visiting crew of aggressive and unpleasant Cardassians. Although they had recently signed a peace treaty with the Federation, the Cardassians had once been Starfleet's bitter enemies. For half a century they had exploited the whole Bajoran people. The Cardassians had built Deep Space Nine as a base to supervise mining operations on Bajor, and they had all but ruined the Bajorans' homeworld. When the planet had been stripped of its minerals, the Cardassians had withdrawn, abandoning the space station.

The Cardassians had reluctantly given up Deep Space Nine to the Bajorans and the Federation. Spitefully they had almost wrecked the station before turning it over to the new owners. Now the Cardassians were supposed to be friendly with the Bajorans. Jake knew, though, that Cardassians still despised Bajorans, and vice versa. A small Cardassian ship under the command of Gul Chok had docked at

Deep Space Nine four days earlier. The lingering hatred between Cardassians and Bajorans had made the four days a tense time for Deep Space Nine and for its commander. "Dad can't help me right now," Jake told Nog. "So I want to ask you to explain these problems to me."

Nog's gaze grew keen with interest. "What's in it for me?" he asked, his voice a little too casual.

Jake couldn't help smiling. This was another way that Ferengi and humans were different. A Ferengi never did a favor without expecting to be repaid in some way. And it would do no good for Jake to remind his friend of the tutoring sessions they had held in the past, when Jake had helped Nog learn to read. That was only human friendship, Nog would say; this is Ferengi business.

"Well?" demanded Nog. "What is it worth to you?"

Jake knew something about Ferengi bargaining traditions. Politely he did not immediately name a price. "What would you suggest?" he asked, giving Nog the honor of setting a high value on his math tutoring.

Nog thought for a moment. Jake got ready to bargain. Ferengi always wanted a profit, but they prided themselves on the give-and-take of haggling. The human boy knew that his friend would demand repayment that was just good enough for him to feel that he had made a smart deal. Finally Nog said, "I've been wondering what Earth is like. Next time you run a holodeck program of Earth, take me along."

"No," Jake said, although he thought that was a

terrific idea. Jake missed his homeworld and often dreamed about going there. Whenever he was able to get some holodeck time, he always ran programs of Earth, where he fished, played an old-fashioned game called baseball, or hiked. The holodeck created flawless replicas of all these things, and when he was using one of the programs, Jake could almost believe that he was really on Earth. It was fun, but a little lonely, because all the people he met in the holodeck were just computer illusions. However, even though Jake wanted Nog to come with him on a holodeck adventure or two, he had to say no because he would insult Nog by giving in too soon. "I'll let you come along on a Mars program instead," he offered, knowing Nog would turn down that compromise.

"That isn't good enough," Nog returned. He was obviously enjoying himself. "I'll help you understand algebra and geometry if you'll let me use an Earth program with you."

Now it was Jake's turn to give in. "Well," he said, "all right. But not just any program. I'll let you come along only on a hike through the Rocky Mountains."

Nog frowned. Like most Ferengi, he was not fond of exercise. "I refuse," he said. "Now, if there is something less strenuous, we might have a deal."

It was time to wrap everything up. With an air of reluctance Jake said, "I suppose I *could* let you come along on a fishing trip. We wouldn't be exercising. We'd just be floating in a boat on a nice, sunny day, catching fish."

"Could I catch more fish than you?"

Jake considered this request. "I don't know about that."

"Three more," Nog insisted.

"Two," offered Jake.

"But mine will be larger," said Nog.

"Okay," Jake agreed. "It's a deal."

Nog laughed. "Great," he said. Then, looking slightly puzzled, he said, "Just one thing: What are *fish?*"

"I'll explain later," Jake told him. "Let's do the math first."

Nog pulled his seat closer so he could see the computer screen and said, "All right. Which problem are you on? Oh, that one. Now, think: What are you trying to find?"

"How far the wheel will roll if it revolves completely two hundred and fifty-five times."

"Good. We'll call that X. Now, remember your geometry—" Nog leaned forward and Jake did, too. Slowly, as his friend explained the connections between the numbers, Jake began to understand.

Finally he said, "Oh, now I get it. What I should be doing is finding the circumference of the wheel. Then I—multiply, right?"

"Right!" Nog said. "Try that."

Jake entered the formula and the numbers. The screen flashed a warm message to him: "Yes, Jake! That's exactly right. Now try this one." Another problem came on the screen.

With Nog's help Jake worked his way through all fifty problems. The homework took more than an hour, and when at last Jake switched off his padd, he finally felt as if he had started to understand a little about math. "Great," he said. "Hey, why don't we get something to eat? I'm hungry."

"All right," Nog said. "As long as we eat at Uncle Quark's."

"Is that a good idea? Won't Rom separate us?" asked Jake. Rom was Nog's father, and he usually sent Nog to his room if he caught the two friends together. He regarded Jake as a bad influence.

"That's all right," said Nog. "My father's away on a purchasing run, and my uncle won't mind if people see us in public there—especially if you pay."

"All right. It's a deal," Jake said.

But Nog insisted that they leave the arcade separately. Jake went first, strolling out into a crowded Promenade. He entered Quark's place, and in the restaurant section he was pleased to see his teacher, Keiko O'Brien, at a table with her daughter, Molly. Keiko was a human of Japanese background, with kind brown eyes and black hair. She took her duties as schoolteacher seriously. Her daughter, Molly, was about three years old. Right now, Keiko was eating some rice-and-vegetable dish with chopsticks. Molly was airpainting.

Molly had a holodisk on the table in front of her, and it sent up a clear column of light. When Molly swept her hands through it, the light changed colors, to brilliant red or yellow or blue, or any combination. Molly was making a three-dimensional painting—of what, Jake could not tell. It looked like a pumpkin balanced on a metal cylinder, but she was changing it as he watched.

"Hello, Jake," Keiko said, looking pleased to see him. "Want to join us?"

Jake smiled at her. "No, thanks. I'm waiting for Nog. I finished my math homework."

"Good for you," Keiko said with a laugh. "I told you that you could understand it if you just kept trying." Beside her, Molly began to chatter away. She could be a talkative little girl, and she often had conversations with herself.

Nog came in, and Jake waved to him. "We'll sit over there," he said, choosing a table close to Keiko's. "I don't think it would be good for Nog to sit with three humans at once."

Keiko gave a wry smile. "I know what you mean," she said.

Nog joined him and, after a glance around, said hello to Keiko. He had attended her school for a while, but his father had taken him out. Nog still liked Keiko, and he even tolerated Molly.

Quark himself came over to the table. "Well, well," he said. "My nephew is with the bad influence again."

Jake and Nog both grinned. Quark, who had long dealt with just about every space-traveling race that passed through Deep Space Nine, was much more easygoing than Nog's father. "I'm trying to teach him to be a good businessman, Uncle," Nog said.

11

Quark shook his head in mock alarm. "Stop giving away our trade secrets right now!" he ordered. "What do you two want?"

"Mmm . . . I'll have a chocolate malted," Jake said. "Nice and thick."

Nog made a face. "Cow juice!" he said in horror. "Uncle, I want a glop, with some Bajoran fizz."

"And who's paying?" Quark asked.

Jake shrugged. "I'll get it this time."

"Most generous," Quark said, and he turned away to get their order.

"Well, Nog, are you keeping busy?" Keiko leaned over to ask.

Nog made a hand gesture that implied, *Yes, but I'm bored.* He said, "I have to admit that I miss school."

"Well, maybe one day you can come back," Keiko said.

Beside her mother, Molly continued to chatter away, just as if she were talking to a real person. She said, "These are your eyes. And this is your chin. And this is your tummy. And these are your funny hands."

Nog frowned. "Does she *have* to do that?" he demanded.

Keiko smiled at him. "She's playing with her invisible friend. Lots of children have them. Didn't you when you were younger?"

Nog shook his head. "No. Ferengi are concerned with the real universe."

12

"Oh, Dhraako is real—to Molly," said Keiko. "She's been talking to him for several days now."

"Dhraako?" asked Jake.

"That's what she says his name is," Keiko said. "He is very tall and thin, and he wears a silver robe with a hood. And his eyes burn like red fire."

Nog leapt up from the table. "No!" he shouted.

People at nearby tables looked up in surprise. In a concerned voice Keiko asked, "Nog, what is it?"

"She sees a Ferengest!" Nog said, staring around the room with wild eyes. "An ancestral spirit!"

"Hey," Jake said, "calm down. It's just something Molly dreamed up, that's all."

Quark was hurrying over, carrying a tray with the boys' order on it. Nog, shaking, stared at the silver shape that Molly had finished sketching in the air above her holodisk. "A spirit!" he shrieked. "Help! Don't let it come near me!" And then he spun and ran. He collided with his uncle. Quark sat down hard on the floor, the tray sailed through the air, and the chocolate malted landed right on Quark's bald head. Nog paid no attention but dashed out into the Promenade. In a moment he was gone.

With chocolate malted running down his face, Quark got to his feet, glaring at the mess. "Someone's going to pay for this," he said. "And I think it's going to be my nephew. What did he—" Quark broke off, his eyes wide as he stared at Molly's air sketch. "A Ferengest!" he said with a sharp hiss. Then he, too, turned and fled.

13

Jake and Keiko stared at each other. Then they looked at the form that Molly had doodled. It looked a little like a skinny humanoid, dressed in a silvery robe. A hood shaded the face, but two red eyes glared out. Molly glanced up and smiled. "Dhraako's gone now," she said. "He followed Nog." Then she touched the holodisk, switching off the image.

CHAPTER 2

Before Jake could follow his friend, Keiko shook her head in exasperation. "What mischief is Nog up to now, Jake?" she asked.

Jake shrugged. "I don't know. He's going to be in trouble when Quark catches him, though." Jake turned to his teacher. "What did they say about a—a Ferengest, was it?"

With a sigh Keiko admitted, "I didn't understand it. Another one of Nog's pranks, I suppose."

A waiter had come out to clean up the mess. Suddenly Jake was no longer hungry. He hurried out into the Promenade, looking for any sign of Nog. The Ferengi boy was nowhere to be seen among the crowds of Bajorans, humans, Vulcans, and others. After a moment of hesitation, Jake turned and made his way toward Operations, where his father's office was. Jake's mother had died years before, and Commander Benjamin Sisko was trying hard to act as both mother and father to Jake. Though Jake knew how busy his father was, the big, forceful man always had time—or made time—to talk to his son.

Jake spoke to several of the station's crewmembers as he approached his father's office. One of them, his father's Bajoran aide, stood against the wall near the office door, looking angry. She was the auburn-haired Major Kira Nerys, who once had been a Bajoran freedom fighter when the brutal Cardassian overlords were busy stripping Bajor of all its natural resources. Now she represented Bajor aboard Deep Space Nine and helped the Bajorans in their exchanges with the Federation.

"Hi, Major," Jake said to her. "Is Dad busy?"

"Very," she snapped. "He's dealing with some garbage."

Jake blinked. "Huh?" His father took care of many things aboard Deep Space Nine, but refuse recycling wasn't one of them. "What do you mean?"

With a toss of her head Major Kira said, "I'm sorry, Jake. Those Cardassian traders—that's what Gul Chok's crew call themselves, anyhow—are negotiating to use Deep Space Nine as a way station for their mineral freighters. And I'm worried that Starfleet will go along with the deal."

Jake swallowed. During the Cardassian occupation of Bajor, Major Kira had fought the Cardassians in many bitter battles, and she was not the type of person to forgive and forget. "Do you think he'll have time to see me?" he asked in a small voice.

"Maybe," the major said. "I only left because I needed some fresh air." She tilted her head and gave him her cool, direct gaze. "You have a problem," she said.

Jake grinned. "You're pretty sharp." After a moment he added, "Do you happen to know anything about Ferengi?"

"Enough to count my fingers after shaking hands with one," replied Major Kira. "Seriously, what do you want to know?"

"Well—Nog mentioned something about a 'Ferengest.' I've never heard of it before, and I wanted to find out what it is."

With a laugh Major Kira said, "Knowing Nog, it's probably a new way to set off a stink bomb in the Promenade." She glanced at the office door, sighed, and said, "Come on. I don't have anything better to do."

She led Jake to a computer console. "Computer," she said, "access data storage, xenobiology section, topic Ferengi, subtopic Ferengi language."

"Working," the computer said, and in a moment it added, "Ready."

"All right, Jake," she said. "It's all yours."

As Major Kira walked back toward Ops, Jake slipped into the chair in front of the computer console. "Computer," he said, "please identify Ferengi word *Ferengest*."

The visual display immediately showed a caped, hooded figure with a huge head, glowing orange eyes, and a menacing attitude. The computer said, "A *Ferengest* is an ancestral spirit. In Ferengi folklore, a Ferengest is a vengeful ghost that haunts its descendants when they violate Ferengi customs or ethics. An unfortunate clan haunted by a Ferengest has bad luck in all of its dealings. Its fortune dwindles and disappears. Other Ferengi shun and ridicule the haunted family, until the Ferengest spirit is appeased by repentance and sacrifice. In extreme cases, clans may be utterly destroyed by the Ferengest."

Despite himself, Jake could not help grinning. A Ferengest was some kind of *ghost?* He did not believe in ghosts, spooks, or spirits, and he was surprised to find that Nog did. With a critical eye Jake looked at the image of the Ferengest. He had to admit that it looked a little like the childish figure that Molly had sketched—but only a little.

The computer said, "An amplified discussion of Ferengi mystical beliefs and practices is available. Would you like to access that, or would you care for a list of related topics?"

"No," Jake said. "That's all."

He got out of the seat and went back toward his father's office. The door was open now, and Major Kira was nowhere in sight. Jake walked up to the door, saying, "Dad?"

He paused just inside the doorway. His father was standing behind his desk, an ominous expression on his dark face. Before him stood three straight, stiff figures—Cardassians. Their plated skins were flushed with emotion, and their heavy necks were stiff with anger and pride. No one noticed Jake. He sensed that an argument was going on. "We know our rights," one of the Cardassians was saying hotly. "We have signed a truce with the Federation, and our request for storage and docking facilities at Deep Space Nine is a reasonable, peaceful one. You cannot legally deny us—"

Sisko brought his hand down on the desk with a sharp report. "You haven't been listening, Gul Chok," he said, his tone deadly calm. "Deep Space Nine is *not* a Federation installation. It is a cooperative venture with the Bajorans. I have no authority to agree to anything without the joint approval of the Federation and the Bajoran government—"

"A government of slaves!" responded the Cardassian. "You can't seriously pretend that these— these insignificant grazing animals have an equal voice with Starfleet—"

Sisko's dark eyes flashed. He held up a hand, cutting off the Cardassian in mid-rant. "Understand this!" he snapped. "The Federation regards all sentient species as equals. I will not have you stand in my office and make racist remarks—"

Another Cardassian interrupted: "*Your* office? May I remind you that we Cardassians constructed this station? Some of us regard Starfleet as little more than a pack of thieves who stole this valuable installation from its rightful owners."

With a visible effort Sisko controlled his temper. "I assure you," he said coldly, "I am constantly aware that Cardassians designed and built this station. I am equally aware that your people left it in a state of—shall we say—marginal operational capacity? Despite your government's assurances that you would turn the station over to us in perfect condition, we occupied a stripped, disabled facility that—"

"This is beside the point," the leader of the Cardassians objected.

Sisko turned away. When he faced the Cardassians again, he had regained his composure. "You are right, Gul Chok. Very well. I will transmit your application for use of Deep Space Nine to both Starfleet and the Bajoran government. Then they will have to confer and reach a mutually acceptable agreement. The decision will probably take a few days."

"We will give you half a day," said the Cardassian. "If you refuse us this concession after that time, I shall report to my government that Starfleet is failing to honor the strict terms of our treaty. I cannot speak for my government, but personally I would consider such behavior an act of war."

A hand suddenly clamped onto Jake's shoulder, and he yelped in surprise. The person who had grabbed him roughly thrust him forward. "A spy!" rasped a harsh Cardassian voice. "A human spy—perhaps an assassin!"

Sisko moved around his desk with the grace and menace of a panther. "You will take your hands off my son," he said, his voice a deadly whiplash of controlled anger.

"I say he is a spy!" the Cardassian repeated. "And Cardassians do not surrender spies—"

"I think it best," said a level voice, "if you do what the commander requests. Otherwise, I shall deal with you myself."

The hand released Jake's shoulder.

Sisko said, "Come here, son."

Jake hurried to his father's side. The Cardassian who had seized him was standing straight, his expression wary. Behind him stood a huge, muscular man,

Chief of Security Odo. Odo took a step back, and with a soft squishy noise, his body melted, shimmered, and re-formed into its normal size and shape. Odo in reality was much shorter and slighter than he had made himself appear.

"Thank you, Odo," Sisko said.

"Only my duty, Commander," responded the shapeshifter. "Shall I escort these . . . gentlemen to our guest quarters?"

Drawing himself up, the Cardassian captain said, "We would not feel secure aboard this station, among spies and traitors. There is an old Cardassian saying, Commander. 'A warrior sleeps but poorly in an enemy's tent.' My crew and I will continue to sleep aboard our ship." To Sisko, the captain added, "Remember, Commander, you will have twelve standard hours before I file my report. I would advise you to consider the possible results most carefully." He strode out, and the other three followed without even a backward glance.

Beside Jake, Sisko relaxed. "Whew!" he said. "Of all the hardheaded, abrasive characters—"

With his hands behind his back, Chief Odo said, "I have arranged for Security to escort the Cardassians back to their ship, Commander."

Sisko shook his head. "I don't think they would care to be escorted, Odo."

"Oh, they won't be aware of the escort," Odo said. "But it's in place, all along their route. If they should leave that route, my people will remind them—gently

—of the path they should take to their docking station."

With a grin Sisko said, "Thank you very much, Chief. And thanks for coming to Jake's rescue."

"I was only doing my duty," repeated Odo. "Will that be all?"

"No. I'll want to make some special arrangements for station security with you—but first I have to get this Cardassian request in shape for transmission." Sisko held up a datapadd, a computerized recording device a little more sophisticated than Jake's school padd. "Wait outside, and I'll be along in a moment."

"Very well, Commander."

When Odo had gone, Sisko turned to Jake. "Son, you picked a bad time to visit," he said with a hint of reproach.

Jake felt a mild regret. "Sorry, Dad. I wanted to talk to you about Nog—"

"I don't have time right now, son. As you heard, the Cardassians are being a little—well, let's be kind and say they're being insistent." He tapped the computer log. "Now you'd better run along. I have to take care of this right away."

"But Nog's acting strange," insisted Jake. "He—"

"Nog is *always* acting strange," Sisko said. "That's part of the peculiar nature of a Ferengi. What's Nog done this time? Changed the food replicators so that chocolate malteds come out as puréed slug slime? Scrambled the communicators so when you call Keiko you get Lieutenant Dax? Made a hole in Odo's sleeping pail?"

"No, he—"

Sisko held up a hand, cutting Jake off. "I'm sorry, son. I'm really busy. Later, all right?"

Jake sighed. "All right," he said. "Sorry."

"I'll see you tonight."

Chief Odo was just outside the office. As Jake passed, the security chief said, "Nog didn't really put a hole in my sleeping pail, did he?"

"Well, no," Jake said. Everyone knew that the chief of security was, in his natural state, a kind of glistening liquid protoplasm. He could change his body to resemble almost anything. Most of the time he maintained a basic humanoid shape to deal with the residents of Deep Space Nine, but when he slept at night, he reverted to his liquid form. If the pail he slept in did have a hole in it, Odo could seep out and ooze all over the floor before he woke up. That would be very messy. Nog hadn't put a hole in Odo's pail.

He had only talked, once or twice, about trying to do it.

"Odo," Jake said, "do you know anything about Ferengi?"

"A little," Odo said. "Enough to keep an eye on that shady character Quark, anyway."

"Have you ever heard of a Ferengest?" Jake asked.

Odo frowned slightly. "Hmm. A ghost of some sort, I believe?"

"Do Ferengi really believe in them?" asked Jake.

"I suppose it depends on the Ferengi," replied Odo. "Most humans do not believe in ghosts—am I correct?" When Jake nodded, Odo continued: "However, if a skeptical human were put in surroundings that were—what is the word?—spooky and told that a ghost would appear, I imagine that the human might have some apprehension."

Jake nodded thoughtfully. He could see Odo's point about skeptics and ghosts. It would be easy even for someone who did not believe in ghosts to imagine all kinds of terrors. After all, nothing is more frightening to a person than his or her own imagination—or nightmares. Jake said, "You mean that most Ferengi don't *really* believe in Ferengests, but they're still a little afraid of them, anyway?"

"Precisely," said Odo. "However, I would also point out that you might have a problem believing anything that Nog says."

Jake felt a little embarrassed for his friend. Nobody seemed to believe Nog—well, to tell the truth, maybe Nog did play too many pranks. Still, the Ferengi boy deserved at least a little consideration, and he had looked genuinely frightened. Well, no matter what anyone else thought, Jake decided, he would give Nog the benefit of the doubt. "Thanks, Odo," Jake said.

"Not at all," Odo replied. He waited until Jake was almost to the door, and then he said, "Oh, Mr. Sisko. One last thing."

Jake turned. "Yes?"

"Please give Nog a message for me. Tell him that if I should by chance seep out of my bed tonight, I will pay him a personal visit. And if he thinks that Ferengests are frightening, he will find the shape *I* intend to take memorable indeed."

CHAPTER 3

Jake searched for a long time, but he could not find Nog. There was one way of searching that he did not try. Although only official station personnel wore communicator badges, everyone who lived permanently on Deep Space Nine carried locators, miniature devices that allowed the computer to lock onto them. Jake could have asked the computer for his friend's location, but Jake knew that if Nog could not be found without using the computer, it was because the Ferengi boy did not wish to be found. After all, Jake thought, it was important to respect a friend's privacy.

Still feeling puzzled and a bit left out, Jake finally went to the quarters he shared with his father. After first ordering a snack from the food replicator, Jake went to his bedroom and settled into a chair to read. He loved to munch peanut-butter bars and drink milk while reading a book.

He summoned up a history of baseball on his

computer screen and read for a while. The game had not been played in an organized way for many years, but on Earth, kids still played it, and Jake liked to read about the history of baseball. He liked the thought of its being the "national pastime" of a whole country, and the names of the great players were like music to him: Babe Ruth, Hank Aaron, and the greatest pitcher of the twenty-first century, Hiro Osaka.

Jake began to grow sleepy. *Day* and *night* had no real meaning when you lived on a space station instead of a planet, but all the species aboard Deep Space Nine had their own periods of rest. Ferengi needed little sleep, and usually their "night" began well after midnight. The slothlike Alephans, on the other hand, were active for only about two hours a day before their personal night began. As it happened, the day on Bajor was almost the same as Earth's, and so the station was on a twenty-four-hour clock. Jake and his dad usually turned in somewhere between ten and eleven at night.

But this evening might be different. At eight Benjamin Sisko called, waking Jake from a doze, to announce that he would be late. He told Jake to order his own dinner, and not to forget the vegetables this time. Jake stirred himself, ordered from the replicator another chocolate malted and a hamburger with all the trimmings (telling himself that pickles really were a kind of vegetable), and took the meal into his bedroom to eat. He had just finished when he heard the living room door hiss open. "Dad?" Jake called. "I'm in here."

But the quick, light footsteps he heard were not those of his father. Jake started for the doorway. Before he reached it, a panting, shaken Nog burst through. "It's been after me all day," the Ferengi boy wailed, eyes wide with fear. With a glance back over his shoulder, he moaned, "Jake, hide me!"

"Uh—sure," Jake said. "Come on into my room." As soon as Nog had rushed past, Jake spoke an order sealing the door to everyone except his father. "You're safe now," he said. "Hey, sit down. You look terrible."

Nog slumped into the chair in front of Jake's desk. "I've been running from that thing ever since I left the restaurant," he said with a weary groan. "No use! It follows me everywhere."

Jake sat on the edge of his bunk, folding his legs under him as if he were about to meditate. "Come on, Nog. I saw the air sketch that Molly made, and she switched it off just after you ran out. It's all gone."

Nog stared at him. "Not the sketch," he said. "It was the Ferengest itself, the real thing! Didn't you see it?"

"Uh—no," Jake said. "And neither did anybody else. Except maybe Molly, and she just made it up. Did you think—"

"Think!" exclaimed Nog. "Think! I *know* what I saw. It was tall and thin, with a hood, and—ugh— those red, staring eyes. Just like in the stories that Grandma Wagga used to tell me to frighten me to sleep. Jake, what have I done? Why is it haunting me?"

"Hey, hey," Jake said. "Calm down. First of all, tell

me about this thing. I don't know much about Ferengests."

Nog licked his lips. "Could I have something to drink?" he asked. "I've been running all day."

"Sure." After unsealing the door, they went into the living room, where Jake ordered a Bajoran fizz from the food replicator. In a moment a tall glass of blue liquid appeared. Trying to hold it away from him, Jake took it out of the replicator. It smelled like old gym shoes, but Ferengi thought it was delicious. He handed the cold glass to Nog.

The Ferengi boy took several greedy gulps. The drink seemed to calm him down. At last he said, "Ferengests are ghosts of the ancestors. They live in the world of spirits, and they never trouble the living —except when one of their descendants has done something very bad, very stupid, or very destructive of profits." He drained the glass, burped, and said, "What have I done? Do you think going to a human school would make my ancestors so angry that they would punish my whole family? How could my schooling have poisoned our profits? My uncle Quark is richer than ever, and I've never done anything to—"

"Calm down, will you?" said Jake before Nog could get all worked up again. "Hey, come on. Do Ferengests ever go for kids in these stories you've heard?"

"All the time!" wailed Nog. "If a kid is in a game and fails to cheat his opponents, they haunt him! Whenever a kid is in trouble with his parents and doesn't lie to get out of it, the Ferengests are waiting to ruin them all!"

"Well, I'm pretty sure no Ferengest is waiting to ruin your family," Jake said. "Look, maybe it's all your imagination. Molly has this invisible friend, and she drew a picture of what he's supposed to look like. Maybe it just happened that the picture looked a little like what a Ferengest is supposed to. That accidental resemblance could have startled you, and then you imagined you saw it pursuing you. That's possible."

Nog got up and walked unsteadily to the food replicator. He replaced his glass and ordered another Bajoran fizz. After he had drunk half of the slimy, bubbling blue liquid, he said, "I see what you mean, Jake. But I don't think so. I ran all through the Promenade, and when I turned around, I could see that monster's eyes watching me, towering up above the crowd. Then I hid out in a turboshaft, but I saw the horrible eyes glowing at me from the dark. So I ran to Constable Odo's office—"

"Wait a minute," Jake said. "You didn't punch a hole in his bed, did you?"

Nog shook his head irritably. "Of course not. Fear before pleasure. I went to his office to see if he would help me, but he wasn't in. And as I was going out, I swear I saw those eyes staring down at me from the level above."

Jake thought for a moment. "Look," he said at last, "you think the eyes are red, right?"

"Orange-red," agreed Nog, shivering. "Hideous, unblinking, staring eyes."

"Okay," said Jake with a calming smile. "There are lots and lots of red lights all over Deep Space Nine. Did you ever think of that?"

Nog relaxed a little. "That's right! Cardassians designed the station, and they see farther into the infrared than most species. So all their warning lights and operational signals and directional signs are red. Do you think I was so scared—uh, I mean, so excited that I could have mistaken some ordinary marker lights for that spirit's eyes?"

With a shrug Jake said, "It's possible. I mean, you were very—*excited*—when you ran out of the restaurant."

"Sure," Nog said, a relieved smile spreading over his face. "Of course. That must be right. After all, I've always been greedy. Often I have lied and cheated and stolen. That's all normal for a Ferengi—maybe even above average. You're right, Jake—what could I have done that would be so bad that a Ferengest would haunt my family?"

"Nothing at all," Jake said.

"Nothing at all," echoed Nog. "You're right. Boy, do I feel like a poor merchant! I'm practically a grown Ferengi. I should have more ears than to be frightened like that."

"You've got great ears," Jake said. "It's just that you were surprised, that's all." He thought of something else and decided to stretch the truth just a little. "I'll tell you something you don't know. When your uncle Quark saw Molly's sketch, he was just as, uh, *excited* as you were. In fact, he was so startled that he threw

33

our order up in the air. My chocolate malted landed right on top of his head."

Nog laughed. "I wish I could have seen that!" he said. "What joy, to see one's elders humiliated!" Then he became more serious. "Uncle Quark! I'd better go see him right away. He won't be pleased with me. Jake, could you do me a big favor? I can't pay for it right now, but when I am able—"

"Hey, it's okay," Jake said. "Humans like to do favors for other people, remember?"

"You're right," Nog said. "I was so carried away that I forgot how unreasonable you are. Very well. Let's—" Nog stopped short. With a trembling finger he pointed toward thin air. He yelped, "Look! Look there! It followed me!"

Jake stared in shocked disbelief. The living room lights had dimmed automatically at nine o'clock. Now, in the darkness, he could just make out a shimmering, transparent silver form, taller than his own father but so slim it looked emaciated. The face was in darkness, beneath what seemed to be a hood. The skin on the back of Jake's neck prickled into goose bumps. He could see nothing of the thing's features.

Except two glaring orange-red eyes.

CHAPTER 4

R un!" shouted Nog, bolting for the door.

Jake grabbed the shorter boy's arm. "No!" he yelled. "Wait!" He shivered a little, but he kept his eyes locked on the glimmering, transparent apparition before them. It was just standing there, absolutely still, a couple of meters away, in front of the viewport that looked out on the bright stars of deep space. Jake thought it stood watching them. At least the two reddish-orange glows that seemed to be eyes remained fixed on them. Nog tugged desperately, trying to rip himself free of Jake's grasp, but Jake held on tight. "Nog! I don't think this is a ghost. Look at it closely."

"That face," Nog said, sounding sick. "And I can see right through it!"

"*What* face?" Jake asked. He could see nothing, only a black blank where a face should be. In fact, except for the vague outline and the eyes, he could see no details at all. "Nog, stop trying to pull away! Look,

a Ferengest would be scary and threatening, wouldn't it?"

"It is!" shouted Nog.

"No, it isn't. This—creature is just standing there. I don't think it wants to harm us."

"Not you—me." Nog at last stopped trying to tear away from Jake's grip. "All right," he said miserably, speaking to the spectral form. "You have me, Ferengest. Show me what penance I must make."

Slowly the apparition raised an arm—at least, Jake thought he could see the misty outline of an arm moving in something like a lazy wave. The arm moved oddly, as if it had three joints, not just a wrist and elbow. Swallowing hard, Jake waved back with his free arm. The hooded head tilted. The creature had noticed that Jake was imitating its actions. It moved the arm again, slowly beckoning to the boys. "Look," Jake said. "It wants us to follow it."

"Into the Spirit World," Nog said. "Where no one makes money and everyone is forced to be honest, generous, and miserable for all eternity."

"Nog, stop it," snapped Jake. "I can't see much of this thing, but I'll bet it isn't a Ferengest at all. It's much too tall." Jake took a deep breath. He decided that he had no time to waste with Ferengi mystical beliefs. "It wants us to go with it," he said. "I say we follow it."

"I—Jake, I'm afraid," Nog confessed in a shaky voice.

His eyes still intent on the figure, Jake said, "All right. I'll follow it, then. You find someone—your uncle, or even better, my dad. Let people know that there's a transparent alien on board Deep Space Nine. I'll try to stay with it. The computer can track my locator signal, so they'll be able to find us. Now, are you calm?"

"Yes!" shrieked Nog.

Jake winced. "I am going to let go of you," he said deliberately. "You move away, slowly. If the creature starts to follow you, we'll make a run for it. If it stays with me, then go and find some help. Do you understand?"

"Find help," Nog repeated. "I'm ready. Let go."

Carefully Jake released his hold on Nog's arm. The Ferengi boy edged away, very slowly indeed—so slowly that Jake guessed he was almost paralyzed by fear. Then he moved a little faster. Still the transparent shape did not move. "I'll find help," Nog called again. Then he dashed through the door, into the corridor, and out of sight.

"All right," Jake said, a little more loudly than necessary. "Can you hear me?"

The ghostly shape made no sign.

"I will go with you," Jake said. Speaking loudly and with precise pronunciation, Jake added, "I trust you." He took one wary step forward. The transparent figure's arm rose and beckoned again, and the creature floated toward the door. Jake followed it. Without removing its red gaze from him, the figure drifted slowly away, and Jake matched it step for step. The door opened as Jake drew near, and they went outside into the corridor. In the brighter light the creature almost faded completely. But by squinting, Jake could just make it out. It led him to an unused corridor, where only emergency lights glowed, and then he could see it a little better.

The alien halted next to a turbolift and pointed at the control panel. Jake hesitated. The Cardassians had thoroughly wrecked the space station before they turned it over to the Bajorans and the Federation. Chief O'Brien had worked hard to get the automatic doors, airlocks, and other mechanical systems functioning again.

Jake wondered if this lift was operating normally. Hoping that Nog would hurry, he touched the keypad. A whine of machinery told him the car was coming. After a moment the lift doors opened. The light in the car chose that instant to flicker and go out. The spectral form of the creature glided inside. Gathering all of his courage, Jake followed the transparent form. The doors slid shut. Jake took a deep, shuddery breath, hoping that he had not made the worst mistake of his life.

The lift began to move.

When he left Jake and the Ferengest behind, Nog's first impulse was to run, wildly and blindly. He was sure that he had made a narrow escape from a terrible fate. If the young human stupidly wanted to offer himself as a substitute sacrifice, so much the better for Nog.

However, something else went into this equation. Jake was Nog's best friend.

Once that would not have meant much to Nog. Ferengi were used to solitary lives, brought up to believe in treachery, deceit, and falsehood as the best ways to deal with one's friends. But Nog, like his uncle Quark, had been learning that the strange ways of humans and others might offer more meaningful rewards than gold-press latinum, dilithium, or credits.

And so, once his initial panic had subsided, Nog paused to consider what he should do. He hesitated to go to Quark, knowing what a scolding his uncle would give him. Nog was a little afraid of Commander Sisko, who towered over him like a great giant. He thought of Security Chief Odo, but he knew that he would have a hard time convincing the suspicious shapeshifter of anything. Nog imagined that if he told Odo that space was dark and full of stars, the security chief would look out a viewport just to be sure.

That left Keiko O'Brien. Although Ferengi believed that women should not teach boys, Nog secretly liked Keiko. She was smart, kind, and—he had to admit—extremely attractive. Where would she be at this time of night?

Nog guessed that she would be in her quarters. Molly was only three, and small human children slept a great deal. He knew where the O'Briens lived, and he hurried there, a furtive small figure easily eluding the glances of the security crew. He finally reached the O'Briens' door and touched the doorbell pad.

Almost at once the door slid open. Chief O'Brien, his curly light-brown hair rumpled, stood before him. "You?" he asked. "What are you doing here?"

"Who is it?" asked Keiko's voice from inside.

Chief O'Brien said, "It's Nog—hey!" With the quick twisting movement of a snake, Nog had dropped to the floor and slipped past him. O'Brien grunted in surprise and reached out to grab Nog—missing him by inches.

Keiko and her husband had been enjoying a meal before a holographic fire. In its flickering yellow light Nog danced around the table, just out of O'Brien's reach, and said, "Teacher, you have to help Jake!"

"Miles," Keiko said to her husband as O'Brien tried again to grab Nog, "let him alone. Jake? What's wrong with him?"

Nog looked from O'Brien's angry red face to Keiko's expression of concern. "A—a Ferengest has him!" Nog gasped.

"A Ferengest?" O'Brien asked. "What the devil's that?"

"It's a kind of ghost," Keiko said. "Nog mentioned it earlier today, and I looked it up this afternoon. Nog, is this some kind of trick?"

"No, I swear on my hope of profits! I—I stake my ears! It's the truth, Teacher."

"Sit down and tell us about it," Keiko said.

It took several minutes, but at last Nog was able to tell the story so that the O'Briens could make some kind of sense of it. "And he was standing in front of the Ferengest in his quarters when I last saw him," Nog finished. "He said to tell someone there was a transparent alien aboard, so I came to you."

Chief O'Brien tilted his head. "A ghost made off with him, then? Is that what you're saying?"

"A Ferengest," Nog said.

The O'Briens looked at each other. "Perhaps you should check it out," Keiko said.

"I suppose so," O'Brien agreed. To Nog, he said, "All right, then. Get up and come along with me, and we'll take care of Jake. But if I find this is all a wild-goose chase, I'll have a word or two with your father about you. Understand?"

"There are no wild gooses," Nog said. "Only Jake and the Ferengest."

"Geese," Keiko corrected. She said to her husband, "Are you going to call Commander Sisko?"

"I think I'd better see him in person," O'Brien replied. "Those Cardassians have been raising all sorts of trouble, and he may be in conference. It'll only take a few minutes. Keep my food warm for me."

"All right."

Nog left with O'Brien, but when they reached the Promenade level, O'Brien said, "Now go along home with you. It's late for a boy to be about. I'll take care of everything."

Nog walked away, but as soon as he was sure O'Brien was no longer looking, he turned and darted along the Promenade, following the chief engineer. It was not that Nog did not trust O'Brien, but he knew how fantastic his story must sound to anyone who did not believe in Ferengests. He wanted to assure himself that Commander Sisko would really do everything he could to find Jake and help him escape from the clutches of that terrible, transparent monster.

They were almost to the lift that led to the Ops level when a shouting, swearing mob burst out of one of the shops. Nog danced back as a cursing Cardassian swung a huge hand at a smaller Bajoran. More Bajorans came running to join the fight, and from somewhere more Cardassians arrived. In an instant the brawl swept between the distant O'Brien and Nog. In another instant the fight became a riot as it spread to the rest of the crowd. Odo's security crew came running from all directions, phasers drawn. Deciding that he had enough trouble to deal with already, Nog darted away, fleeing by an emergency route that only he knew.

The clanky, creaking turbolift shuddered to a halt. For one terrifying instant Jake was sure that the doors had malfunctioned and that he was trapped in this lightless coffin. Then, with a weary hiss, the doors opened, and a little light leaked in. Jake had no idea where he was. The lift had gone down, toward the lower core area of the station. That part was all engineering, power, and systems control, but like the rest of the station, it was not all repaired. The section that he stepped out into was another one that the Cardassians had ruined. Wall plates dangled from wires and tubing, and only a dim orange-red glow from the emergency lights gave any illumination.

As soon as he was out of the elevator car, Jake looked back for his ghostly companion. For a moment he could not see it at all. Then he realized that what he thought was a reflection of one of the emergency lights really was the glow of the creature's eyes. Jake squinted and half turned his head, looking at the figure from the corner of his eye. That technique worked when he was looking for an especially dim star in astronomy class, and it helped a little here. Yes, there was the barely visible mistiness of the hood and shoulders, the spectral shimmer that marked the creature's body. The form moved slowly forward. Jake stepped aside to let it pass, and then on impulse he reached out to touch it as it came up to him.

His hand plunged through empty air, but he felt something, a sensation of prickly coolness. The creature drew itself up and turned to glare down at him. "S-sorry," Jake stammered, yanking his hand away. "I won't do that again."

After a moment the creature backed away, beckoning. Jake followed it, shuffling his feet in the dark to avoid any unpleasant surprises like loose deck plates or scattered debris. Through the floor he felt a constant humming vibration, and he guessed that he was not far above the fusion reactors. He knew that only two of the six reactors were functional. The Cardassians had disabled the rest before they turned the station over to the Bajorans and Starfleet. Those disabled reactors were potentially deadly sources of radiation. O'Brien had shielded them all, though, and he had made sure there was no direct way to approach them.

"Where are we going?" Jake asked, but the gliding figure ahead of him gave no sign.

Jake raised his hand to activate the emergency homing signal of his locator, but then thought better of it. He was sure that Nog would somehow get through to his father. He was not sure what the creature might do if Jake suddenly summoned help. Jake could imagine all sorts of reactions from the "ghost" if a security crew should burst in, brandishing phasers. Maybe it would attack. Maybe it would disappear. Maybe—Jake could not help smiling at the thought—a few humans would frighten the "ghost" away!

He lowered his hand and followed the transparent figure's slow progress. It came to a hatchway, one of the ponderous Cardassian gear-toothed security doors, and somehow it activated the sensor, because the door rolled away. Jake stepped through the hatch. He was in a room that once, perhaps, had been a repair or manufacturing station. It was about six meters square, with dim blue light coming from the ceiling panels. In even that much illumination, the "ghost" faded out completely. Jake stood uncertainly for a moment. Behind him the door sealed itself again. With a puzzled expression Jake sniffed the air. It smelled funny, a sharp electrical scent that was a little like ozone, as if he were breathing a mixture slightly adjusted to someone else's biological requirements.

After a moment the lights dimmed and turned red-orange. Jake looked about him. Was that the "ghost?" Yes, it was: The familiar transparent shape stooped over a control panel built into one wall. It had turned down the light so that Jake could see it. It faced him and beckoned again. Jake started toward it. "Look," he said, "I don't want to complain, but this is getting pretty boring. Where are we off to now?"

The specter held a hand up—or at least, the sleeve raised, again bending strangely, as if the long arm had an extra elbow. Jake could not see details well enough to be sure that a hand was sticking out of the end of the sleeve. "You want me to stop?" he asked. He did, standing still. After a moment the transparent shape made a pushing gesture. "Back?" Jake asked. He took one step backward.

Then the figure wanted him half a step to the left, then half a step forward again. Jake began to feel exasperated. "I don't know what you're doing," he complained. "If this is some kind of—of ghost folk dance, I don't particularly want to learn it. Now what?"

The creature seemed satisfied with Jake's placement at last. It drew something out of its robe and pointed it toward him. Jake saw a twinkling starburst of light, and then—

An explosion!

He yelped and closed his eyes as a hot flash of light burst around him. The deck seemed to shiver under his feet, and a hot whiff of ozone burned his nose. He felt for a sickening second that he was about to faint, that everything was whirling around him. Then the moment passed.

Cautiously Jake opened his eyes to glaring light.

Standing before him was a tall figure in a silvery-gray robe. Its deep-set red eyes glowed from a dark gray face. Its smooth surface had no trace of a nose, but there was a down-turned mouth. From the sleeve of the robe issued a skeletal arm, ending in a bony hand that grasped a device made of coppery spheres, crystal rods, and shimmering lights. The hand lowered the device, and the surrounding glare faded to a more bearable level.

As soon as it did, Jake yelled in terror.

Deep Space Nine had vanished.

A billion stars shone in fierce, undimmed brilliance all around him.

And in the depths of space, he and the creature were standing on nothing.

CHAPTER 5

The fight in the Promenade was sharp but short. Odo himself came to the scene to sort things out. The Bajorans loudly claimed that the Cardassians had begun the fight, and the Cardassians in turn objected that the Bajorans had attacked them for absolutely no reason at all. In the end the security crew escorted three Cardassians and five Bajorans to Ops. Nog watched all this from a perch on level two of the Promenade, and when he was sure the coast was clear, he set off for Ops himself.

He got there just moments behind the security crew and the rioters. Standing against the wall with his arms crossed, Miles O'Brien was waiting outside Commander Sisko's office. However, Security Chief Odo's mission apparently was more important than O'Brien's, because the head of station security escorted his prisoners into the office. A few of the station's crew watched them go and murmured questions to one another about exactly what had happened. Nog worked his way over to O'Brien and asked, "Did you tell him?"

O'Brien gave him a surprised look. "I thought you'd gone home to bed. No, I haven't told Commander Sisko yet. He was on subspace communication with Starfleet when I arrived, and then this riot broke out. But I promise I'll give him your message just as soon as—"

"Oh, oh!" It was the voice of a young ensign over at the Operations table. "Chief, you'd better come and have a look at this. According to the readout, all docking ports just lost primary power."

"What!" O'Brien's red face grew even redder as he hurried over and gave the computer status screen a quick, expert glance. "Bloody Cardassian bucket of bolts! I see what you mean. All right, Ensign Jonas, I'm on it. Have a maintenance crew meet me at the main power juncture on the docking ring in five minutes. Probably just the bloody power-relay sensors malfunctioning again, but we'll have to make sure."

"Wait!" Nog called. "What about—"

O'Brien shook his head. "Sorry, Nog. I have a job to do. Look, this shouldn't take long, and that lot in the office will probably keep the commander busy for a little while, anyway. As soon as we've repaired the docking port power, I'll be back, lad. Now, don't worry, Nog. I'm sure everything will be all right." To the ensign, O'Brien barked, "This won't wait all night, you know! What about that repair crew?"

"On the way, sir," responded Jonas.

O'Brien hurried away, leaving an angry and frustrated Nog. He slyly glanced around. No one was looking at him. He edged over to Commander Sisko's office door just as a furious-looking Cardassian in a captain's uniform came striding toward it. The door hissed open, and when the Cardassian marched inside, Nog slipped right in behind him, completely unnoticed. He immediately lost himself in a dark corner and became all ears—not a hard task for a Ferengi.

"This is an outrage!" the newcomer roared at once, the huge, ropy tendons in his neck swollen with strong emotion. "Sisko, if your people can't even guarantee my crew's security against an unprovoked attack by a vicious pack of—"

"Quiet!" snapped Sisko, his voice raspy and irritated. He looked tired, edgy, and ready to hit someone. "Gul Chok, more angry words won't help the situation. The fight is over, and no one was injured— fortunately. As to the question of who started it, we are in the process of settling that right now, so don't be too quick to assign blame." He turned back to Odo. "Chief Odo, continue your report."

With a glance at Chok, the shapeshifter said, "As I was saying, Commander, the witnesses make it plain that Barys Kavar struck the first blow."

"After having been goaded by those bullies!" objected one of the Bajorans. "Commander, their race enslaved mine for decades, treated us worse than animals. To sit so close to this monster, to hear his foul insults was more than I could stand—"

Commander Sisko held his hand up for silence. "Exactly what did he say?" he demanded.

The Bajoran looked defiantly at one of the Cardassians, who smirked back at him. "He called us sheep!" exclaimed the Bajoran. The others murmured in angry agreement. Standing as tall as he could, Barys added, "I don't have to stand for that."

With a sigh Commander Sisko said, "And do you happen to know what a sheep is, Mr. Barys?"

"Of course!" sputtered the enraged Bajoran. "Everyone knows that a sheep is—well, a—it's a kind of—and who wants to be called one, anyway?"

"I thought so." Sisko turned to the Cardassian captain. "Very well, Gul Chok. I cannot say your crew were blameless in this—this incident, but I cannot find them guilty of anything more serious than childish behavior. In fact, both sides have behaved like brats. I propose that we release all these prisoners, on the condition that they agree to avoid each other."

"Poor discipline, Commander," growled Chok. "However, I agree to the compromise. My men will take some refreshment at that Ferengi place. Have these—sheep—go elsewhere."

One of the Bajorans stirred, but a security man placed a warning hand on his shoulder. Sisko nodded. "Then go now, and take all your crew with you."

"Only six hours left before the deadline, Commander," said Chok. "I trust my answer is coming."

"For the last time, I will not tolerate ultimatums," replied Sisko. "The question is before Starfleet and the Bajoran government now. I've put everything in motion. I suggest you do the same." The commander glanced meaningfully at the door.

"Come," ordered Gul Chok. He turned and left the office. Slowly, in single file, the insolent Cardassians strutted out behind him, unpleasant grins on their faces.

"And these Bajorans?" asked Odo, with a gesture at the five remaining prisoners.

Commander Sisko sighed. He rubbed his eyes. "First, let me tell them a little about sheep. Barys, sheep are—uh, noble Earth creatures. They are noted for, uh, their solidarity and their use to humankind as providers of wool, a fabric that protects the elderly and the young from the elements. I would suggest that you Bajorans ignore any such meaningless taunts from the Cardassians in the future, since the Cardassians clearly do not know what they are talking about."

Barys looked a little puzzled, but at last he nodded. "Believe me, Commander, the last thing we want to do is to encounter those—those unmannered, ignorant, savage animals again. But this space station is supposed to be a joint venture of your people and mine. If you allow our old enemies free run of the place, then my government will be most displeased."

"Tell it to get in line," said Commander Sisko with a sour expression. "Go on now, and keep out of trouble."

The Bajorans headed toward the door, and Nog slipped out from his hiding place—but not fast enough to escape Odo. The security chief said nothing, but he grasped Nog's arm with a firm grip and escorted him out. "The commander is too busy to speak to you at the moment," he said.

"Please," Nog groaned. "This is really important. It's about Jake."

Odo tilted his head. He did a good job at maintaining a humanoid form in general, but he tended to let little details slide. His ears, for example, were merely two smooth pink shells—and in Nog's opinion, far too small to make him really impressive. He said, "What about Jake?"

"He's in trouble. Chief O'Brien was supposed to tell Commander Sisko," Nog said.

Odo looked at the Ops table. "Where is Chief O'Brien?" he asked Ensign Jonas.

The busy ensign turned away from his monitors. "We're showing a major power failure in the docking ring. Chief O'Brien has taken a crew to repair it."

With a nod Odo asked, "Before the chief left, did he say anything about Jake Sisko?"

The ensign looked baffled. "The commander's son? No, sir."

"Thank you, Jonas. That is all." With a displeased expression on his face, Odo shook his head. "Nog, I hope this will be a lesson to you. You'd better start planning your tricks more carefully if you ever hope to fool anyone. Now leave. We're entirely too busy for your pranks right now. If I catch you in Ops again, I am going to be severe." As if he had just thought of something, Odo added, "In fact, just to make sure you stay out of trouble, I'll escort you back to your uncle. Now, come along with me before I find some regulation your family has violated and close Quark's den of iniquity."

It was an effective threat. Nog tagged along beside Odo, feeling more frustrated than ever. Didn't anybody believe him? He considered going back to Keiko, but she'd just try to turn things over to O'Brien again. After a moment of indecision Nog made up his mind. He would have to speak with his uncle.

On their way to the restaurant, Nog noticed an unusual number of security types around. Odo's people blended in, but they nodded as their chief passed, and he gave them curt nods in return. Odo must have warned his crew to keep a sharp eye out for trouble. As the two got close to Quark's place, Nog slowed his pace. Something was wrong. At this time of night Nog's establishment was a loud, boisterous den of revelers and gamblers—usually. But tonight everything seemed strangely quiet. "After you," Odo said as they got to Quark's place. Nog knew he wasn't just being polite. The chief of security was all too aware of how quickly a small, agile Ferengi could slip away the minute no one was watching.

Inside, Quark stood behind the bar, looking unhappy. "There you are!" he called out as soon as they entered. "I knew you would come."

After a moment of surprise Nog realized that his uncle was not even talking to him but to Odo. "I am returning your nephew," Odo said coldly. "He strayed into a place where he does not belong. I trust you will see that for the next day or so he remains in his quarters and out of trouble. Good night."

"Wait!" Quark squawked. "A moment of your valuable time, if you please, friend Odo."

Nog glanced around with some curiosity. Now he saw the reason why the place was so deserted: The Cardassians who had left Ops a few minutes before had joined more of their kind. A dozen or so of them lounged at the tables. No wonder the place was empty. No one wanted to revel with Cardassians.

"'Friend Odo?'" asked the security chief in a voice dripping with sarcasm. "That's a new one, Quark. It has always been my impression that the minimum requirement for friendship is that two people like each other."

"Oh—I like you, Odo, I really do," objected Quark. He blinked, probably realizing how incredible that declaration sounded. Hastily he added, "Or at least I hold the very deepest respect for you and the job you do."

Politely, with a bored smile, Odo murmured, "Even if you try to violate every rule the moment my back is turned. A strange kind of respect, Quark."

With a despairing glance at the Cardassians, Quark said, "We can't talk here. Please, just a moment, Odo. I ask you—as a favor."

"Well," Odo said, sounding really impressed. "If

55

you're that desperate, Quark, I can give you just a moment, no more."

Nog followed the adults into his uncle's office. The door slipped closed, and Quark collapsed into his chair, moaning. "They are ruining me!" he complained.

"Who?" asked Odo.

"The Cardassians!" exploded Quark. "No one else will eat or drink here!"

"Have the Cardassians broken the law?" Odo asked, some interest flickering in his voice.

"They're breaking *me!*" Quark said.

Odo asked, "But what are they doing?"

Quark flapped his hands in a gesture of angry helplessness. "They're driving customers away and ruining my business. My receipts are down to almost nothing!"

"You are serving the Cardassians food and drink," observed Odo. "I assume that they, at least, are paying you."

Quark pounded the table. "They're cheap!" he howled. "A Cardassian will nibble for hours at a miserable puckerplum salad, and they're drinking nothing but plain, inexpensive water!"

Odo sighed. "Quark, I will be glad to arrest every last Cardassian in the place—"

"Thank you, thank you, friend Odo!" Quark bounded up from his chair, reaching to grasp Odo's hand. "If there's ever anything I can do for you—"

"Let me finish." Odo yanked his hand away. "I will be glad to arrest every Cardassian in the place the moment they break a law. Until then, however, they are your problem."

"But what am I supposed to do?" ranted Quark.

With a thoughtful expression Odo said, "You might raise the price of puckerplum salad. Good night— 'friend' Quark."

The security chief left. Quark sank back in his chair, glowering at Nog. "Up to mischief again, are you?" he demanded.

Nog could not meet his uncle's eyes. "Jake's in trouble," he muttered.

"We're all in trouble," returned Quark. "And it's all the fault of those miserable, tight-fisted Cardassians."

"Uncle," pleaded Nog. "Jake needs our help."

Quark put both hands to his head. "Jake, Jake, Jake!" he shouted. "That's all I ever hear from you! You know your father doesn't approve of that human boy. Why don't you find some normal Ferengi friends for a change?"

"I'm the only Ferengi of my age on the station," objected Nog. "But that's not important right now. Jake himself saw the Ferengest—"

With a hiss Quark made a complex sign with his fingers, an ancient Ferengi gesture meant to ward off evil influences. "That's another thing," he said. "You with your nonsense about Ferengests and haunts and I don't know what else! I don't need any more trouble from you. Until these Cardassians are off the station, I want you to stay in your quarters. Do you understand that?"

"Uncle—"

Quark waved his hands wildly. "I revoke your rights of free passage! I rescind your contract of freedom of movement! You are to stay confined to your quarters until further notice. You are bankrupt of the coin of freedom! You are—you are—what is that Earth term?"

"Grounded," Nog muttered.

"You are grounded!" Quark thundered. "I have spoken! By the profits of my ancestors, if you show your ears outside your room before you have my permission, I'll have them both for soap dishes!" Quark pressed a pad on the desk, and after a moment a private security man, a tall, scaly green Valpasian, came in.

"Yes?" he hissed in his soft reptilian voice.

"Vissh, my nephew is to go directly to his quarters. Take him there and see him inside. I will arrange a change in the exit code myself."

"Uncle—"

"Go," Quark ordered. "Now I've got to protect my investment. Maybe I could spread a rumor that puckerplum salad causes one's neck to shrink—"

"Come," said Vissh. He laid a cold hand on Nog's shoulder.

Defeated, Nog went along quietly. Valpasians were a skinny, green species that had descended from a race of intelligent lizards, and they were quick and keen-

eyed. He would have no chance of giving Vissh the slip.

Still, Nog knew, he had to find some way of helping Jake.

He wished he had some faint idea of what that way might be.

CHAPTER 6

With a strangled cry Jake threw his arms out and revolved them like a windmill as he tried to regain his balance. Before him, the now-solid "ghost" hovered beside a strange chest-high device shaped a little like a mushroom. The hooded creature held out its device of spheres and rods—and a voice, coming from this contraption and not from the creature's lips, spoke softly: *This form will adjust solidity for more comfort.* The voice had an odd, nonhuman tone, halfway between male and female. It added, *Close eyes, please.*

Closing his eyes was one of the hardest things that Jake had ever done. The vast emptiness of space terrified him, and he had the awful feeling that if he shut it out, he would open his eyes to discover himself alone and dying in the cold vacuum between the stars. But he forced his eyelids closed, and for a terrible minute he seemed to float in an infinite, lonely blackness. Then light burst against his closed eyelids, bright enough to make him see a vivid red, and he felt a humming, droning vibration. He took a deep, shuddering breath of that ozone-scented air.

Open now. Is done.

Trembling, Jake opened his eyes. He blinked. Now the life-form in front of him was almost transparent again. The station, however, had come back— partially. It, too, was somewhat transparent. Jake stood on a deck that was like fogged glass, and through it he could see the piping, support struts, and machinery that kept the life support functioning. He gasped at the brilliance of several "rivers" of multicolored light. Dazzling blue-white streams gave birth to bright yellow tributaries, which fed to orange branches, which finally gave way to very small networks of reds and purples and magentas. "What's that?" Jake gasped. "All those colors!"

The tall, humanoid creature turned its head to look at the rivers of light. *That is energy flow of station power generators to all servo-mechanisms.* Turning back toward Jake, the creature made the speaking device ask, *That form is now functional?*

"Huh?" asked Jake. "Uh—do you mean am I all right?"

Am I all right? said the creature.

"I don't know," Jake said. "Are you?"

After a moment of silence, the creature waved its speaking device again. *Explain I, you.*

Jake's head swam. "Well," he said, "I am, uh, me. Jake Sisko." He patted his chest. "This form is I."

Then am I all right?

Jake laughed. "No, no," he said. "When you speak, *you* are *I*. I become *you*."

The creature inclined its head. *Ah. You and I are a Whole. This form understands.*

"I—I don't think you do," Jake said. "Look, I guess I'm okay. But what's happened? And who are you?"

You are I.

Jake shook his head. "No, let me ask it differently. Who is that form?" He pointed to the creature.

Ah. Comprehended. This form is a Dhraakellian Quester, an expression of the Dhraakellian Whole. That form is—hu-man?

With relief Jake said, "Right, I am a human. My name is Jake Sisko." Remembering Molly's invisible friend, he asked, "Are you—are you Dhraako?"

The glaring red-orange eyes could not blink. They had no eyelids. But they suddenly seemed meditative. After a moment the creature moved its speaking device, and it said, *The small one that sees and hears calls this form that. It could not comprehend the nature of the Whole. That is why this form has brought Jake Sisko here. Jake Sisko must help this form.*

"Uh, does that form mind if I call it Dhraako?"

This form minds not.

"Okay, Dhraako," Jake said. "I'm glad to meet you. What are you, exactly?"

This form is exactly an expression of the Whole.

"Man," Jake moaned. "This is gonna take a *long* time."

It did. Little by little Jake pieced together an amazing story. Dhraako was not really an individual, he gathered, but more like a part of a greater organism —an organism that was an entire species called the Dhraakellian Whole. Just as different parts of the human body served different functions, some of them circulating blood, others digesting food, and others seeing, hearing, smelling, touching, and tasting, so the different expressions of the Dhraakellian Whole were like organs. Questers, Jake gathered, were a sort of combination of eyes and ears. Their job was to observe the universe, somehow feeding the information they gathered back to the Whole.

Jake asked, "Where do you come from? How did you get here?"

With practice Dhraako was getting the hang of conversation. At first its dark-gray face had held no readable expression, but Jake saw that his impression had been mistaken. In fact, the flesh of the face was incredibly mobile, and the down-turned mouth quirked and wriggled as the cheeks swelled or shrank and the eyes glowed darker or brighter. He could not understand these strange expressions, but somehow they made the Quester a little more real and less alien. *We live,* the Quester explained, *a kind of existence not like yours. This here-and-now is one expression of space-time. We live in another.*

"Is that why we can't see you?" Jake asked.

Yes. We live in a place between this material universe and a plane of pure energy.

"Oh," Jake said. "Like a different dimension?"

Di-men-sion, said the speaking device, as if trying the word for the first time ever. *Yes, dimension will serve. We know your place of existence, but it is cloudy to us. Our science has allowed us to observe. That is the task of this form: to observe and report. None of the large solid peoples can see this form. Only the very young ones.*

"You're invisible to adults?" asked Jake.

In-vis-i-ble, repeated Dhraako. *Yes. This form, Dhraako, does not understand why young can see, old cannot. Jake Sisko is between young and old. Jake Sisko is partly aware of this form. That is why Dhraako must speak to Jake Sisko.*

"I see," said Jake, wondering if he really did. "Are you the only, uh, Quester here, Dhraako?"

The mobile face suddenly gave Jake an impression of enormous age and great loneliness. *Yes.* The ghostly form touched the mushroom-shaped device. *Dhraako came in a Quester ship to this part of the galaxy through the fabric disturbance many of your years ago. All, all alone since.*

Jake frowned. "Fabric disturbance?" he asked. "Is that what we call the Bajoran Wormhole?"

Worm-hole, agreed the device. *Yes. Bridge to other side of galaxy. Where the Whole evolved. This expression, Dhraako, came first here when this station was constructed.*

"By the Cardassians?" Jake asked.

Yes. Dhraako saw them and their victims, those Jake Sisko calls the Bajorans. Dhraako lived invisibly aboard this station to witness and report.

"Wow," Jake said. "You must be really old."

The Whole knows no age, said the device. *But Dhraako knows aloneness. Dhraako felt the pain of the Bajorans. Felt the anger of the Cardassians. Dhraako —hard to say—feels inside that Cardassians wish to destroy. Dhraako does not like destroyment of those Dhraako observes.*

Jake felt uneasy. "I don't understand, Dhraako. Do you mean that Deep Space Nine is in some kind of danger? Now?"

Terrible danger, the speaking device said. Dhraako adjusted one of the spheres, and suddenly the voice increased in volume and urgency: *Jake Sisko! This station will be destroyed! All aboard will die! This happens soon!*

"What?" Jake asked, feeling his stomach turn over. "Deep Space Nine will be destroyed?"

All aboard will die! Must help give warning to save those forms aboard this station! The Quester leaned forward, its orange-red eyes blazing with intense appeal. *Jake Sisko—you only can save this station!*

If Vissh had been a Ferengi, he might have suspected that something was wrong when Nog went along to his quarters so quietly. Vissh's race hatched their young from eggs and allowed them to grow up on their own. Vissh had never had to deal with a young person. So he went his way sure that Nog was safe and sound and locked in.

That was only partly true. Nog was safe, all right, but as soon as the door hissed closed, he tried immediately to open it with a stern verbal order. The door did not move. Nog had hoped that Quark's difficulties with his unruly Cardassian customers would distract his uncle from his threat to change the door codes, but Quark had remembered. It was time for Plan B.

Nog went to his bedroom. Rom, Nog's father, tried to be a good Ferengi parent. For example, he regularly searched Nog's room to find anything that Nog might have hidden. To keep him happy, Nog concealed lots of small items in easy-to-find places: a lost ring he had found that bore an Altairian flame gem, a platinal coin he had sneaked from a careless gambler's winnings, and other little tidbits. And he always protested loudly and angrily when Rom confiscated these.

But that was only for show. In his *real* hiding places, Nog kept some treasures that Rom never found. He opened a light module. He switched off one of the light globes and removed it. Nog regretted having to break the globe, because figuring out how to get the replicator to duplicate the globe right around his special find had been very difficult. However, he was desperate, so he carefully wrapped the globe in a permasheet and smashed it. Then he retrieved his prize from the shards. He reprogrammed the food replicator to recycle the broken light globe and fabricate a new one, then replaced it in the module. Then he set about his escape.

Nog's Uncle Quark had one treasure that he valued above all others. It was a set of Cardassian isolinear chips. These computer components could override any computer commands that required security clearance. After weeks of careful planning, Nog had stolen one chip from his uncle's supply. He plugged the chip into the computer terminal and ordered, "Computer override Quark's order and open the portal of Rom's living quarters immediately!"

The door slid open and Nog dashed through. He felt a strong pang of regret. Quark would be sure to guess how Nog had opened the door, and he would demand the return of the stolen isolinear chip. Still, Nog thought, his uncle would have to admire his cleverness in stealing and using the chip. He hoped it would all balance out somehow. He took a twisting route that only he knew back to Ops. This time he was determined to see his mission through.

Almost as soon as he arrived, the commander came out of his office, with Odo close behind. "They are annoying us on purpose," Odo said. "We will have no peace on Deep Space Nine until you order those Cardassians off the station."

"Odo, I can't," said Commander Sisko. He looked brutally tired. Nog realized the commander had been awake for almost twenty-four hours. The big man yawned and said, "As you said, we have no reason to arrest them until they break the law."

Odo leaned forward. He was beginning to look tired, too, melting a bit at the edges. "Commander, I have checked Gul Chok's background. He and his crew have no legal standing among the Cardassians. They are little better than criminals, passing themselves off as representatives of their government. Chok may command his own ship, but he has no right to the military rank of 'Gul.' Has it occurred to you that the Cardassians could be terrorists?"

"Of course it has," Commander Sisko said. "Chok and his crew may be a group of space pirates. But Cardassians hang together, and his government is not about to confess to Starfleet that Chok is beyond their control."

"Or perhaps he is not," Odo insisted. "Commander, I know the Cardassians. There is a real possibility that the Cardassian government has sent Chok here on a secret mission of sabotage."

The commander gave Odo a sarcastic grin. "Including wiping out Quark's profits? No, Odo, I really can't see that they've done anything that could seriously harm Deep Space Nine. I assure you, the second that I do—"

Nog took a deep breath. He had concealed himself behind the Ops table. Now he stepped around it. "Commander Sisko," he said. "I have to talk to you."

"You again?" With a disgusted grunt, Odo stepped forward and grabbed his arm. "You will have to learn your lesson more forcefully," he said. "Very well—this time I'll deal with you myself."

"Commander!" Nog shouted desperately. "Locate Jake!"

"Wait," Commander Sisko said to Odo. He turned to a console and said, "Computer, locate Jake Sisko."

After a moment the computer voice replied, "Jake Sisko is not on Deep Space Nine."

Frowning, Commander Sisko said, "When did he leave?"

The computer said, "Jake Sisko is aboard Deep Space Nine."

"Then where on the station is he?" demanded the Commander.

"Jake Sisko is not on Deep Space Nine."

Sisko and Odo looked at each other. Carefully Sisko said, "Computer: Justify your statements about Jake Sisko."

The computer replied, "Jake Sisko is aboard Deep Space Nine. Jake Sisko is not aboard Deep Space Nine."

"Which is true?" yelled the frustrated commander.

"Both," the computer responded.

Drawing a long breath, Sisko said, "Let Nog go, Odo. I think we have a bad situation on our hands."

CHAPTER 7

Walking through the station was like walking through a spaceship made of glass. Through the transparent deck plates, red, yellow, and blue-white stars blazed beneath Jake's feet. He blinked in wonder at the intricate maze of power conduits, sensor cables, and servo devices he could see through the transparent walls. He felt as if he were looking at an X ray of the station. Once or twice he and Dhraako passed a Bajoran or a human, but they never even noticed the two. The misty, dim forms drifted silently past, their features hardly visible.

This way, directed the speaking device. Dhraako manipulated the instrument of spheres and crystal, and with a flash of light everything grew even more transparent. *Come,* said Dhraako. *Move slowly, Jake Sisko. Follow Dhraako.* The Quester sank right into a closed door.

Jake gulped. He inched forward and felt himself oozing right through the closed metal hatch! It was

like passing through a cool, tingly wall of water. "All right!" he said on the other side. "Can we do that again?"

When necessary. Dhraako manipulated the device, there was another flash, and the station became somewhat more visible. Dhraako had led Jake to a narrow ledge in a hollow cylindrical shaft that went straight down.

Jake saw where they were heading. "Wait," he said. "This service tube leads to one of the damaged reactors. The radiation down there will kill us!"

No, Dhraako assured him. *Jake Sisko and Dhraako are perfectly transparent to such radiation.*

It took faith to trust the Dhraakellian, but Jake swallowed and nodded. Dhraako swung to one side and stepped onto a ladder built into the emergency maintenance slot of the lift-tube, and Jake followed. A few red service lights illuminated the tube. Dhraako and Jake had to climb down the emergency ladder because the service lift had been demolished by the Cardassians. Since the tube led only to an unusable reactor, Jake guessed, O'Brien had seen no reason to repair it right away.

Jake had trouble hanging on to the transparent rungs set into a recess that ran straight down the wall of the tube. If he fell, would he smash at the bottom of his fall? Or was he so insubstantial that his body would pass right through the walls and into space? He shivered and continued his long climb, trying not to look down.

They were nearing the ring of Cardassian artificial-gravity generators. Jake remembered hearing O'Brien complain about the primitive devices. In the main body of the station a Federation inertia-damping system had replaced the old-fashioned gravity collars, but so few people came here that O'Brien must have left this one functioning. What would happen when they passed it?

He soon found out. They reached a brief zone of dizzy weightlessness, and Dhraako spun, so that his head was where his feet had been a moment before. The Quester began to climb—to climb "down" from their former perspective. Jake followed him. Very soon he felt the tug of gravity, and then he seemed to be climbing up, even though he was still moving toward the bottom of the station. It was all very confusing.

Jake knew that the huge space station was shaped something like a top with a long central shaft. Three bulges interrupted the shaft. From top to bottom, and from largest to smallest, they were the Ops and Promenade decks, the storage and engineering decks, and finally the fusion reactors, toward the very bottom. The Habitat Ring, where the station's personnel and visitors lived, was attached to the Promenade by crossover bridges, and this extra circle was what gave Deep Space Nine its toplike appearance. The gravity collar lay below the inhabited areas, but above the reactors. That was what Dhraako and Jake had just passed. Now that they were on the far side, gravity had reversed and pulled them "up" toward the collar. The tube led from here right into the dangerous reactor section.

Two white-hot suns blazed ahead. Jake realized that he was seeing into the heart of the two active fusion reactors. He gasped. If he were here in his normal state, unprotected, the radiation would fry him in seconds. Still he felt nothing, and still Dhraako climbed on. Jake imagined the awful feeling of radiation crisping his skin, burning away his hair, cooking him like a steak. It took a lot of determination for Jake to follow the Dhraakellian.

At last Dhraako came to a round platform and

stood there waiting until Jake reached it, too. For a moment Jake stood, arms and legs aching from his long climb, chest heaving as he tried to get his breath. He was not only worn out from the climb but also tired. It had to be past midnight. Then the Quester pointed, extending a long, skinny, triple-jointed arm. Jake frowned. "I can't see anything, Dhraako."

Dhraako will adjust solidity. Close eyes, Jake Sisko.

Again there was that silent explosion of light, and this time when Jake opened his eyes, the station had almost vanished. Dhraako looked very real and solid now, but Deep Space Nine had become a thin ghost of itself. Against the darkness of space, the fusion reactions glared with a fascinating, terrible light, and around them, sketched in the wispiest form imaginable, were the reactors. *There,* said the speaking device.

Jake squinted. The four dead reactors still had fuel in them, and though the fusion reactions had been damped, enough radiation leaked from the cores to make them sullen, angry red balls of light. Close to one of these red glows was a cluster of spheres. They were the size of bowling balls, and they had to be made of something very heavy. They were opaque, dark round shapes against the angry red light of the reactor. Jake counted five spheres, barely touching each other, arranged in a ring. "Yes, I see now. What is it?" he asked.

Dense matter, Dhraako replied. The Quester turned and looked at Jake, its thin, mobile face twitching in expressions that the human could not understand. *Potentially unstable.*

Now that he was looking at the spheres, Jake could tell that they clustered around a pipe that led straight into the heart of one of the dead reactors, although the pipe itself was invisible. "What are they made of? Nuclear fuel?" he asked.

Dense matter, Dhraako said again. The Quester seemed to have some difficulty in framing a concept. *As used by the Cardassians for mining, other purposes. Can be made to release energy suddenly, with violence.*

Jake understood. "A bomb!" he shouted. "You're telling me that there is a bomb in the reactor!"

Destructive device, Dhraako replied. *Left by the Cardassians. One of the ones who placed it there has returned, the one called Chok. This dense matter has been inert. Now one of the Cardassians has caused reactions to begin.*

"A time bomb," Jake said, feeling cold. "The Cardassians have set a time bomb to blow up the station." He reached for Dhraako's arm and found that it had become solid. His fingers clenched on curiously smooth, cool fabric and on the skeletal arm inside. "Dhraako! How long before the bomb explodes?"

Difficult to say with exactness. A matter of a few of your hours. Dhraako's computer is working now to predict exact time.

Jake felt sick and dizzy. "And what will happen if it goes off?" he asked, already suspecting the answer.

Destruction, Dhraako told him. *The station will explode. Those aboard will cease to exist in this here-and-now.*

Everyone would die. "I have to warn Dad!" he shouted.

Dhraako worked Jake Sisko's transformation to Dhraako's dimension to warn Jake Sisko. Jake Sisko must help think of way to warn others, said Dhraako.

"Then put me back," Jake said. "I'll tell Dad, and he—he'll do something! We've got to save the station!"

The Dhraakellian Quester turned, its red eyes strangely sorrowful. *Cannot do, Jake Sisko.*

"What!" Jake yelled.

Cannot put you back in material universe. Only can move from that side to this, not back.

Jake's heart thudded in his chest. He felt ill with fear. Dhraako was telling him that the coming explosion would doom the station and everyone aboard it—and that nothing he could do could possibly prevent the explosion from happening!

"Interesting," Odo murmured. "In the future I shall have to see that this corridor is secured."

Nog rolled his eyes. He and Odo were out looking for any sign of Jake—and he was showing Odo practically every one of his and Jake's secret passages, shortcuts, and hiding places. Now Odo wanted to seal them off. It just wasn't fair! Helping a friend ought to be more profitable than this.

"Sometimes we met here," Nog said, stepping through a doorway. Odo followed him inside. The room had once been a Cardassian junior officer's quarters. Now it had minimal power, enough for lights and the food replicator. Jake and Nog had scavenged enough furniture to set it up as a cozy hideaway with a table, a couple of chairs, and a small computer. The computer had been channeled into the ship's system, and on its screen a menu of games blinked on and off.

Odo nodded. "You have been busy," he said. "Is that a Federation computer?"

"No!" Nog protested. "It's just an old Cardassian model. Nobody wanted it, so we moved it in here to play games on."

Odo touched the screen. The opening instructions of the game Starfleet Commander began to scroll past. "I see," the security chief murmured. "You've tapped into the arcade systems. Very nice. You and Jake can come here and play any game you want and never have to spend a credit."

"But this is just flat stuff," Nog objected. "It isn't like the hologames. That's what we pay for—and we still play plenty of games in the arcade, too!"

"Well, as chief of security, I cannot overlook the theft of services," Odo said. "I'll have to get around to having all this removed . . . some day. You see no sign of Jake here?"

"No," Nog muttered. "I guess you'll have to tell my father and Uncle Quark that I've been stealing game time."

"Don't be absurd," Odo replied. "They'd only be impressed with your cleverness. I won't help you gain their respect."

Oh, well, Nog thought, *you can't blame a Ferengi for trying.* "Come on," he said with a sigh. "You might as well see the other places."

But Jake was nowhere to be found. Nog became more and more upset. "You don't know what it's like," Nog said bitterly. "I don't have any other friends."

To Nog's surprise Odo unbent just a bit to express

sympathy. "I have no friends at all," Odo reminded him. "Still, I can appreciate your feelings, I think. Is this the last place?"

"No," Nog said. "There's one other." He hated to reveal this passageway to Odo, because it was the one that allowed him and Jake to roam between levels of Ops and the Promenade without being detected.

"I thought this was a sealed area," Odo said as Nog led him through an access door.

"It's supposed to be, but the locks and sensors failed. You know what a mess the Cardassians left."

Odo studied him. "The Cardassians—or two young fellows looking for secret passages?"

Nog turned on the security chief, his hands balled into angry fists. "Jake and I found it this way!" he shouted. "Neither of us could disable sensors and locks! But you won't believe that, will you? You won't believe anything I tell you!"

Odo smiled—a very slight smile, to be sure, but a brief and unmistakable smile. "On the contrary," he said. "I believe you . . . now."

"Come on," Nog said. He turned down the darkened corridor, pointedly not even mentioning the loose deck plates. He grinned when he heard Odo stumble behind him. "I guess you'll have this one sealed off, too," Nog called over his shoulder.

"It's a dangerous place to be exploring," Odo replied. "You or Jake could get hurt or—what's that noise?"

Nog froze, his huge ears practically quivering as he listened. He heard the grinding whir of a lift coming from close by. But the turbolifts in this corridor were all broken—weren't they? "It's coming from up ahead," Nog said.

Odo was at his shoulder. "Let's go."

They rounded a long curve of the corridor, with the grinding sound growing louder and louder. Nog halted. "This is the one," he said, pointing to a closed lift door. "It's coming this way."

Odo put his hands on Nog's shoulder. "Quiet," he said. "If this isn't Jake, it could be—" He didn't finish, but Nog could guess his thought: It could be the Cardassians, up to no good. The wait was not long, but to Nog it seemed agonizing.

At last the car rumbled to a halt. With a protesting groan, the long-unused doors shuddered apart, revealing a car bathed in the dim red light of an emergency lamp.

"It's empty!" exclaimed Odo.

"No!" Nog screamed. He pointed with a shaking finger. "Odo, don't you see them? Don't you see Jake? Oh, no! It's happened—*now Jake is a Ferengest too!*"

CHAPTER 8

When the lift doors opened, Jake was almost as surprised as Nog. For a stunned moment he stood beside the Quester, staring at the ghostly figures of his friend Nog and the tall, thin form of Odo. Then, faintly, Jake heard Nog's startled cry and saw him pull away from Odo in terror. "Wait!" Jake shouted as loudly as he could. "Nog! I need your help!"

Too late. The young Ferengi jerked free of Odo's hold and went stumbling and running down the passageway. Jake ran after him, yelling for Nog to stop. He did not know if Nog could hear him at all. He guessed that if he could make any sound that ordinary people could detect, it would be a tiny, faraway noise, like the high-pitched hum of a Denarian smallfly. Nog looked back over his shoulder once or twice with an expression of sheer terror. Jake finally stopped chasing him, and his friend barreled out of sight around a corner. When Jake retraced his steps, he met Odo. The security chief passed him—but suddenly he stopped, turned, and tilted his head, and his lips moved. Jake strained to hear what the shapeshifter was saying. He could barely make out the precise words, "Is anyone there?"

"Yes!" Jake yelled. "Me, Jake Sisko! Help, Odo!"

Odo stood irresolutely for a moment. Then, with an angry jerk, he turned and walked away. The Quester glided silently toward Jake. "No one can hear me," Jake complained.

True, Dhraako's speaking device agreed. *Their sounds are faint to us. Ours they cannot hear—except for the young.*

"That's right," Jake said thoughtfully. "Molly! Can we talk to her?"

The small one can hear. How much she understands, Dhraako does not know.

"She doesn't have to understand," Jake said. "All she has to do is hear what I say and repeat it to Keiko—or to Chief O'Brien. Come on—I know where she lives."

As they moved through the ghostly corridors of Deep Space Nine, Dhraako suddenly activated the speaking device. *Jake Sisko. A possible way of returning you to your universe of material existence has occurred to Dhraako.*

"What?" Jake asked.

It is complicated. Dhraako has witnessed the operation of the device you call a transporter.

"Yes," Jake said. "What about it?"

Dhraako's fingers moved over the crystal rods. *When your body is in transit from one place to another, held in the transporter beam, it is here.*

"Here?" Jake asked. He stopped, and so did Dhraako. The red eyes gleamed. Jake said, "You mean, a person who is transporting is in the dimension where we are?"

Yes. Except the person is here for only an instant, and in that instant the person has no awareness. But if the transporter can put you here, even momentarily—

"If it can put me here," Jake said slowly, "it can take me out of here, too! What do we have to do, Dhraako?"

The features of the Quester flickered. Jake suddenly realized that it probably communicated that way among its own kind, without using sound at all. No wonder it had found human speech puzzling. The thin fingers manipulated the rods of the speaker, and the calm voice said, *There would be much to communicate to those on the other side. If a precise time could be arranged, and if you could be where Dhraako has lived, then the operator of the transporter might be able to locate you, to—*

"To lock on," Jake said.

As you say, to lock on. The transporter then might make you materialize again on the other side. The features of the Quester shifted and rearranged themselves. *At least, that is possible in theory.*

"In theory?" Jake stared hard at the Quester. "What else could happen?"

Reluctantly Dhraako fingered the rods. *Jake Sisko could be lost between this dimension and his own.*

Jake shivered. Lost in a transporter beam—that would be a terrible kind of death in life. He had heard of "transporter dreams," fleeting impressions that a few people had now and then while in transit. No one could explain them, and most scientists believed them to be just illusions. They did not seem to hurt anyone, and normally the few people who had them forgot about them. Jake shook his head. "I guess we'll have to try that," he said reluctantly. "But first, let's find Molly. Come on—she's our only hope of communicating with Dad."

They walked on in silence. It was very late by Jake's time, and he was exhausted, aching for sleep. Still, he realized that the bomb might go off at any moment. He had no time to rest. When they arrived at the O'Briens' quarters, Jake said, "She's in here. I guess we'll have to, uh, thin out to get through the door."

The Quester raised its device, pointed it at Jake, and Jake felt the sickening little twist as the station faded away. He and Dhraako stepped right through the closed door, and then the nursery door. Then Dhraako adjusted Jake's "realness" again, and they were standing beside Molly's bed. The light panels had been turned down to give a soft night-light glow. The little girl lay sound asleep, a teddy bear beside her. Dhraako made his speaker say softly, *Dhraako has never awakened the little one before. Dhraako would not frighten her.*

"I'll do it," Jake said. He crooned, "Molly. Oh, Mollee! Time to wake up. Your friends are here."

Molly sniffled a little in her sleep and turned over on her side. Jake called again, a little louder. For a moment nothing happened, and he was afraid she couldn't hear him. Then she blinked her eyes open, rubbed them with the back of her hand, and grinned at him. "Hi, Jake," she said. Her voice sounded faint and tinny, but he could hear her words, and she could obviously hear his. That was a relief, anyway.

Jake could have hugged her—but he suspected that if he tried, his arms would go right through her. He grinned back. "Hello, Molly. Sorry to wake you up."

"Still dark," she said. "Where's Mommy?"

"We'll call her soon," Jake said. "See who else is here?"

Molly raised herself up in bed and grinned. "Dhraako!" she squealed. "Didn't you like the picture I made?"

The picture was pleasing, Dhraako responded.

"'Cause you ran off. I thought maybe you didn't like it."

"Molly," Jake said, "You're a smart girl, aren't you?"

Molly grinned shyly. "Uh-huh."

"Do you think you could say everything that I say?"

"Is it a game?" asked Molly.

"That's right," Jake said. "It's a game." He hoped that it would be more than that, but Molly was too young to understand. "You know how your Mommy can't see Dhraako?"

"Grown-ups are weird," Molly agreed, wrinkling her nose.

Jake almost laughed. He had to agree with Molly. He had known some very weird grown-ups in his time. "Yeah, they are," he said. "Well, your mommy can't hear me now, either, because I'm where Dhraako is. So you'll have to tell her everything I say. All right?"

"All right," Molly said.

"Okay, call your mother." To Dhraako, Jake said, "Here goes. Wish us luck."

Luck? asked Dhraako.

"I'll explain later," Jake said. "Call your mommy, Molly."

Grinning, Molly yelled, "Mommy! Mommy!"

"Again," Jake said.

Molly liked this game. She screamed out again, and although her voice came thinly to him, Jake knew that she was really bellowing. In a few seconds the lights came up, and Keiko came hurrying into the room, wearing a dark blue kimono and a worried look. She spoke to Molly, but though Jake could barely hear a few sounds, he could not understand anything she said.

"Jake is here," Molly said, pointing.

Keiko crossed her arms. By looking hard at her lips, Jake could just follow what she said: "This is not time to play with invisible friends, Molly. You have to go back to sleep."

"Molly, say this!" Jake yelled. "Jake is in another dimension."

Molly squinched up her nose. "Jake is in 'nother di—dimension," she said, and then she laughed.

"What?" asked Keiko, with a frown.

Jake said, "Molly, say there's a bomb in the reactors."

Molly tried to repeat what he said: "Jake says there's a bob in the tree tractors."

"Molly," said Keiko. "You've been having a dream. Would you like some hot milk?"

Jake groaned. His brilliant idea was not working out. He said, "Molly, tell Keiko that Jake needs help."

"Jake needs help," Molly said.

Going to the food replicator, Keiko said, "Your father has already checked on Jake. I'm sure Jake is in bed, sound asleep. Which is where you should be." In a moment she came back with a glass of milk. "Here," she said. "You drink this down and then go back to sleep."

"He's not a dream," Molly said, sounding disgusted.

"Dreams can seem very real," Keiko replied.

"Mommy! He's right *there,*" objected Molly, pointing.

Keiko swept her arm—and Jake gasped as it passed right through his chest. "See?" Keiko said. "Nothing is here, darling. Now, you drink your milk."

"Sorry, Jake," Molly said.

Jake gave her a sickly smile. "That's all right, Molly. You go back to sleep. Dhraako and I will find some other way."

They left Keiko with Molly. In the corridor Jake

said, "There's only one other person who can even see us. I've got to find Nog. He wouldn't be in any of our usual places, because he thinks that I'm some kind of ghost now. So he'd be close to someone who might protect him. We have to go to Quark's place."

By now it was very late. The last few customers had walked, staggered, or crept out of Quark's bar and restaurant, and a yawning Quark stood behind the bar counting the day's take. Behind him the door to his office was open. Jake and Dhraako went through, and sure enough, there lay Nog in an exhausted sleep on the sofa.

"Do you think he'll be able to hear me?" Jake asked the Quester.

Dhraako replied, *Difficult to say. Perhaps. The Nog form can see Dhraako better than Jake Sisko, but not as well as Molly. Perhaps Nog may hear you if you speak loudly.*

"It's worth a try, anyway," Jake said. "At least it's quiet here." Then, at Jake's suggestion, the Quester made itself so transparent that even Jake had trouble seeing it. He guessed that in this form, Dhraako would be completely invisible to Nog. It would be better if the young Ferengi saw only his human friend, not a menacing ancestral spirit. Satisfied, Jake bent over and called to him, as loudly as possible. Nog's eyes flew open, and he scrambled back into the corner, too terrified even to scream. Jake held up his hands, trying to show that he meant his friend no harm. He smiled.

Nog made a strange gesture with two crossed fingers. Jake thought hard about some way to communicate. He had a sudden idea. He held up one finger of his left hand, then one finger of his right hand. He brought his hands together, lowered his left finger, and held up two fingers of his right hand. Then he did the same thing, except this time he added one finger to two to make three. Did Nog understand him? He was speaking mathematics, a universal language. One plus one is two; two plus one is three; three plus one—

Nog stared. He held up both of his hands and added one to four to make five. He understood—and fortunately, he had caught on before Jake had run out of fingers. "Jake?" Nog asked. By lip-reading, Jake could recognize the word.

"Yes!" he said, exaggerating the word and nodding.

"Are—are you dead?" Nog asked.

Jake shook his head emphatically. "I'm stuck," he mouthed.

"Struck?" Nog asked. "Who struck you? The Ferengest?"

"Not struck—*stuck.*" Jake mimed walking along, and then suddenly acted as if his foot had become glued to the floor.

"Stuck!" Nog shouted. This time Jake could hear his faint voice. "You are alive?"

Jake nodded again. Then he pointed to himself. He pointed to the empty sofa beside Nog.

Nog frowned. "You—you want to get back to where I am?"

Jake grinned and nodded so hard he thought his head would fall off. "Yes!"

Nog scratched his bald head. "You must speak

louder. I can hardly hear you. How—how do you get back?"

Jake could not speak louder. He had been bellowing at the top of his lungs. This called for some real acting. First Jake played a transporter engineer, engaging the controls. Then he dashed across the room, drew an imaginary circle on the floor and stood in it. Then he waved his hands to show that he was shimmering and disappearing. Then he jumped to another place, patted his body, and nodded his relief to find himself solid.

"The transporter!" Nog said. "You need to use the transporter!"

Jake clasped his hands and shook them over his head. "Way to go, Nog!" Then he pointed to an antique Ferengi timepiece that Quark kept on his desk.

"Clock," Nog said. "Hours. A special time? Oh— you have to transport at a special time?"

Nog was great at the game. Jake looked at the time display. Fortunately, Quark had adjusted the clock to follow ship's time. Jake indicated a time forty-five minutes from that minute, and Nog caught on. Then came the hardest part. Jake beckoned to Nog and began to back out of the room.

"F-follow you?" Nog said. "Uh, w-will I wind up like you?"

Jake shook his head.

"I don't know if I ought to trust you," Nog said.

Jake flapped his arms in despair. Then, very deliberately, he pointed at Nog, and then at himself. He clasped his hands before him, then moved them up and down. He was imitating an enthusiastic handshake.

"We're—we're friends," Nog said. He knew of the odd Earth custom of shaking hands. He bit his lip with his sharp teeth. "All right," he said at last. "May the ears of my ancestors hear my plea for protection! Let's go."

Quark looked up sharply as they left. "Nog! I told you to stay in my office! Where are you going?" he barked in an angry voice. "You have to be punished for—"

"Later, Uncle!" Nog shouted, and he, the ghostly Jake, and the almost invisible Dhraako hurried out into the Promenade and ducked into one of the boys' private passageways.

CHAPTER 9

I am impressed," Nog said. "Even *I* have never come down here!" Jake was really getting the knack of lip-reading now, and he could understand Nog pretty well. The young Ferengi had either recovered his self-control or else was doing a good job of hiding his fear. He and Jake stood in the big empty room that Dhraako had used as headquarters, still lit only faintly by the reddish glow of the emergency lights. When Nog walked right through the chest-tall metallic mushroom, Jake blinked. Then he remembered that the mushroom-shaped piece of equipment must be Dhraako's. Jake could see it as more real and solid than anything else in the room, but to Nog, it was invisible. "What now?" Nog asked Jake.

Jake could not see Dhraako clearly in the dim light, but the Quester was right beside him. The unemotional voice of the speaker said, *Show Nog that Jake Sisko will stand where I will stand. The transporter must try to lock onto Jake Sisko there.*

Jake squinted, trying to see Dhraako better. The shimmering humanoid form paused a meter away from the strange metallic mushroom, and then it stepped back. Jake carefully stood in the same place. Again he pantomimed drawing a circle on the floor. He looked at Nog expectantly.

Nog nodded. "I think I have it. You have to be right here in"—he checked his chronometer—"in thirty-six minutes when the transporter activates. You'll stand on that spot there. All right. I have the deck level and the room location memorized. Let's go find your father."

Yes, Dhraako's speaking device told Jake. *You go. Dhraako will stay here to complete computer calculations.*

Jake and Nog hurried along. Time was running out—in more ways than Nog knew. If the bomb had been set to go off before the transporter crew could retrieve Jake, then all was lost. And even if it wasn't, there was a chance that Jake could not be retrieved at all. Then the station would explode, and everyone on it would die. Or would they? Jake wondered what would happen to him and Dhraako. If they could survive the hard radiation close to the reactor cores, would an explosion destroy them? If it didn't, could Jake live in the hostile vacuum of outer space? He began to shake from a combination of exhaustion and dread. That was one experiment he never wanted to try.

Taking every shortcut they knew, Jake and Nog reached Ops level in just over seven minutes. Only half an hour left! They found everything in the operations center in a swirling state of chaos. Jake almost yelled with relief when he caught sight of his father, standing behind the Ops table with a tired and worried look on his usually strong face. Commander Sisko was speaking, and Jake was so familiar with his facial expressions and his way of talking that even before they approached him, Jake could tell what his father was saying.

"O'Brien," Sisko said to a communicator, "have the repairs to the docking circuits been completed?" He listened for a moment to a reply that Jake could not hear. Then he puffed out his cheeks and said, "That's good, because Chok has just informed me that our time is up. Of course, Starfleet and the Bajorans haven't replied to his ultimatum, but Chok won't listen to reason. His ship will depart in five minutes." Another pause, and then Sisko grinned without much real humor. "I agree with you: Good riddance to them."

Major Kira, looking irritable and grouchy from lack of sleep, came up beside Sisko. "Commander," she said, "the Cardassian vessel is signaling that it is ready to go. Security reports that the Cardassians have left the station and are aboard the ship. All of Chok's crew are accounted for."

"They have permission to leave dock," Sisko said. Then he tapped the communicator again. "Odo," he said, "any trace of Jake?" Jake watched his father's face fall. "Well, continue the search. Blast it, he *has* to be somewhere aboard!"

"He's here!" Nog shouted.

Everyone froze. Sisko jerked his eyes off the readout board and stared at Nog. "Here? Where?" he demanded.

Nog pointed. "You can't see him," Nog said. "He's stuck. But I know how to get him back."

A security man took a step forward, but Sisko put out his arm and held the man back. "I don't know what you mean by 'stuck,' but how can we get Jake back?" Sisko asked.

"You have to set a transporter to the coordinates I will give you and look for Jake's locator signal," Nog said. "And you have to do it in *exactly* twenty-four minutes."

Sisko tapped his communicator. "Chief O'Brien, meet me in the main transporter bay at once," he said. Then to Nog, he added, "You'd better be telling the truth."

Nog ignored him. He turned to Jake and said, "Go, now! Hurry! I'll wait on the transporter side."

Jake nodded and ran back along the passageway. He hoped that everything would work. If not—

Well, if not, he did not even want to think of what might lie in store for him and for Deep Space Nine.

A few minutes later Nog stood before a hologram, a three-dimensional sketch of the deck level where Jake had taken him. He placed a finger on a spot almost in the center of one compartment. "Here," he said. "Jake will stand right here."

Nog and Jake's father had met O'Brien in the

transporter bay, and O'Brien had tapped into the computer to call up the hologram. Now Commander Sisko looked at the chief engineer with an inquisitive expression. "A fabrication room," O'Brien explained. "It's where the Cardassians used to assemble personal weapons. Since accidents happen, particularly with Cardassian design systems, the room's a heavily shielded compartment, out of the way and not of much use. As far as I know, it's vacant."

"Can you lock onto this coordinate?" Sisko asked.

"Certainly," O'Brien said. "I ran the transporter array on the *Enterprise* for years. If Jake's there, I'll bring him back."

"Four minutes left," Nog said.

Commander Sisko's communicator chirped. "Ops to Commander Sisko," said Major Kira's voice.

"Sisko here," acknowledged the commander.

"Sir, you'd better come back here, on the double. There may be trouble brewing."

Commander Sisko looked angry. "What is it now?" he demanded. "Make it short, Major."

"Sir, the Cardassians aren't leaving."

"That's ridiculous. They've already gone, Major. They departed before I left Ops!" Sisko said.

Major Kira's tone was earnest: "Yes, sir, but the Cardassians merely withdrew on impulse power. They're about ten thousand kilometers away now, and they're just hovering there."

"What?" Sisko said. "What do you mean, 'hovering'?"

"Just what I said, sir. They're dead in space, as if

they're just watching us." After a brief pause Major Kira added, "As if they're waiting for something to happen."

"Major Kira, scan them. See if their shields are up," Commander Sisko ordered.

"Yes, sir."

Nog tugged at Sisko's arm. "Two minutes!" he said, his voice high with excitement.

"I know," Sisko said. "O'Brien, get ready."

O'Brien moved to the control panel of the transporter and adjusted the settings. "Yes, sir. I'm setting the coordinates."

Again Major Kira's voice chirped from Sisko's communicator: "Sir, they have not raised their shields."

Sisko said, "Then they are offering no threat."

"No." Major Kira sounded as if she were reluctant to make that admission. "But, sir, they're up to something. They must be. Cardassians can never be trusted. I repeat my request: You should return to Ops immediately."

Nog said, "One minute!"

Sisko said, "I'll be there shortly, Major. Continue to monitor them. Do not, repeat, do not attempt to hail them or to undertake any defensive action that they might misinterpret. As soon as we have Jake back, I'll come straight to Ops."

"Sir, is it wise to delay?"

"Major," said Sisko, "calm down. I know you don't trust Cardassians, but there's no rush."

"Now!" yelled Nog.

Chief O'Brien activated the transporter.

Jake had arrived at Dhraako's quarters with just a few minutes to spare. The Quester was still there, making some adjustments to a control panel atop the strange mushroom-shaped mechanism. Dhraako looked up and nodded a greeting as Jake came in. "Are you ready?" Jake asked.

After a final adjustment Dhraako produced the speaker. *All is ready, Jake Sisko. If everything proceeds as Dhraako wishes, you will be restored to your own people in seven and a half of your minutes.*

Jake nodded. "I see. I—I suppose we won't be able to talk to each other after the change."

The Quester's face reshaped itself in another of the creature's unreadable expressions. *That is correct, Jake Sisko. But you are a part of the Dhraakellian Whole now. You will forever be a part of the Whole.*

"How?" Jake asked.

In memory.

"Oh." In spite of his anxiety, exhaustion, and worry, Jake smiled. "I guess you will always be a part of me, too, Dhraako. I'll never forget you."

This form is honored.

"Yeah," Jake said, a little embarrassed. "Well, so am I."

A bright blue light flashed silently on the top of the metal mushroom, and Dhraako leaned close to study it. Suddenly the Quester straightened, urgently fingering the speaker. The artificial voice again came out with an edge of distressed excitement: *Jake Sisko! Dhraako's computer has calculated the time the bomb device will explode! It will be very soon!*

"How soon?" Jake asked, fighting a wave of panic. "How long do we have?"

The Quester moved its long, thin, bony fingers with lightning speed across the top of its display. Jake could see no letters or figures, and he heard no computer voice, but a bewildering constellation of colors flickered and flashed as light displays flared all over the surface of the mechanism. Some pulsed in frantic red, others twinkled from green to orange, and still others shone with combinations of blue or violet. Gripping the mechanism with one hand, the Quester fumbled for the speaker with the other. *Jake Sisko! The bomb device will explode within three point five two of your minutes after the transporter activation!*

"Three and a half minutes!" Jake was stunned. What could he possibly do in so short a time? It was hopeless.

The Dhraakellian was staring hard at Jake with those huge, glowing eyes. *Jake Sisko! A chance of survival! Dhraako's ship will take both of us to safety if we leave now! What is Jake Sisko's decision?*

Jake thought of abandoning Deep Space Nine. He felt like crying. He still remembered how his mother had died in a savage attack by the mechanized Borg. Was his father doomed, too? And his friend Nog, and all the others aboard the station? "No," he said.

"Dhraako, save yourself if you can, but I—I have to be with my family and friends. No matter what happens."

After a moment the hooded head inclined in a graceful nod of assent. *This form understands. Ready yourself, Jake Sisko. Time of transportation is very near.*

"Dhraako—just in case I—I don't see you again, I want to thank you. For the help you've tried to give us."

The Quester's head bowed. The voice from the speaker was slow, with perhaps a hint of sorrow. *This form thanks Jake Sisko. Even if we both survive, this form can never see Jake Sisko again. Dhraako must leave Deep Space Nine.*

"Leave?" Jake asked. "Why?"

The thin fingers moved over the crystal rods, and the voice explained: *It is against the wishes of the Whole that a Quester becomes known to those who are watched. It is only because of the great distance to the Whole that this form has been able to speak and act with Jake Sisko. This form must leave the station and seek other kinds of life elsewhere to observe.* The head raised, and Jake thought he could see sorrow in the large red eyes. *Dhraako will be forever mindful of Jake Sisko. Dhraako has learned much here of the concept of friendship.*

"You've been a friend to me," Jake said. "To all of us. Thank you again."

The Quester straightened, all business, alert and

tense. *Ready now. Time is very near. Close eyes, Jake Sisko. Dhraako says farewell!*

Jake tapped his locator to send out a homing signal, then squeezed his eyes shut. This time the silent explosion of light was much more intense, and it lasted longer. He felt a prickle of heat all over his skin, and then the familiar tingle of the transporter beam. Then all was silence, darkness, and fear.

"Do you have him?" asked Sisko, his voice shaking with emotion.

Behind the transporter controls, Chief O'Brien sweated. "I've got *something,*" he said. "I'm picking up a faint locator signal. This is difficult. It's like an attempt to transport at extreme range. I'm boosting the gain now."

"Is it Jake?" Nog asked.

"Losing the signal," O'Brien said. "Hang on. I'm going to match the pattern with Jake's. He's used this transporter before, so his body pattern should be in the buffer. If I can hold this one until I retrieve Jake's, I can use it to amplify—there! Got it." O'Brien's big but surprisingly delicate hands flew over the controls, adjusting, coaxing, trying to drag the pattern out of thin air and into reality. At last the big Irishman looked up with a gleam of triumph in his eyes. "Yes, it's Jake! Hold on, lad—here goes nothing."

The transporter pads pulsated with strong surges of power. A glittering pattern began to form, faded, came back again more strongly, and then shaped itself into a

sparkling human outline. "Got him!" O'Brien yelled, and a second later Jake Sisko stood swaying on the pad, looking out at them with wide, dark eyes.

"Son!" Sisko shouted, stepping forward with his arms outspread. "Where in the galaxy have you—"

"No time!" Jake said. "Chief O'Brien, check the sensors for a mass of dense material just above one of the dead reactors. The Cardassians left a bomb there —and it's about to explode!"

CHAPTER 10

Where?" demanded Chief O'Brien. "I can't find it, Jake, if you can't point out exactly where I have to look."

Jake studied the hologram of Deep Space Nine with desperate attention. He knew roughly where the bomb had been placed—but roughly was not good enough. O'Brien did not have time for a full scan of the fusion reactors, and anyway, the radiation would make precise readings difficult. The holographic model of the station floated right before Jake's eyes, but he was having trouble finding the precise spot where Dhraako had showed him the bomb. "It looks different," he said. "How much time's left?"

"Only a minute and a half," Nog said. "Quick, Jake. How can we help?"

"It looks so different this way," complained Jake. He felt grimy and dizzy from lack of sleep. His eyes burned. If only he could see the station the way he had while in Dhraako's dimension, he thought—yes, that was it! To O'Brien, Jake said, "Can you make the hologram more transparent? So that I can see through the plates and things?"

"Right away," O'Brien said. He adjusted the hologram. It faded until it was like a model made of glass.

Jake bent in for a close look. Yes, that was it. He traced a cooling pipe with his finger and then pointed dramatically. "Right there!" he said. "It's a group of five spheres, clustered right around this pipe."

"Scan that area," ordered Sisko.

"Right away, sir," said O'Brien. He directed the scan from the transporter station. Grimacing in concentration, O'Brien said, "Nothing . . . nothing . . . no, here it is! Five foreign bodies, just where Jake said."

Sisko was sweating. He wiped his face with his palm and said, "Chief, is there anything you can do to disarm the bomb?"

"Half a minute!" Nog said.

O'Brien shook his head. "Negative. But I *can* lock on with the transporter controls. With that much mass, the transporter won't be able to fling it far, but maybe a few thousand kilometers will be enough." He manipulated the transporter board. "I'm putting all available power into this," he warned. "Here goes!"

The transporter hummed. Sisko tapped his communicator. "Ops, put the Cardassian ship on the screen," he said. "I want to see their reaction if we pull this off. Prepare to raise shields on my order." Just then the

lights dimmed and faded, and even the artificial gravity lessened. Jake felt strange, as if his weight had suddenly decreased by half.

"It's away!" O'Brien yelled as normal power returned.

The auxiliary screen came to life, showing the Cardassian ship waiting in space. Almost at once, halfway between the station and the Cardassian vessel, a searing burst of energy appeared, like a white-hot new star close by. "Raise shields!" ordered Sisko.

Jake watched as a red, spherical shock wave expanded from the blast. It came closer and closer—

"Shields up," reported Major Kira's voice.

The shock wave hit. The lights dimmed again, and the screen dissolved into ionic static. Then, after an anxious moment, the screen wavered back to life, the lights came up, and everyone exhaled. "We're still here," said Sisko. "Major Kira, scan the Cardassian ship."

"Scanning . . . Commander, they've taken shock damage to their central power controls. The ship cannot raise its shields or go to warp speed. Wait . . . Chok has engaged his impulse engines. I think he's trying to run away."

Sisko nodded and said, "Major, dispatch two runabouts to intercept that vessel. Arrest Chok and his crew on Starfleet authority."

Even if he had not already known how much Major Kira despised the Cardassians, Jake could have guessed it from the satisfaction in her voice: "Yes, sir. Right away."

Sisko turned to Nog. "You were a great help," he said. "I won't forget that."

"Then tell my uncle not to punish me," Nog replied. "That would be the best way of not forgetting!"

With a grin, Sisko said, "I'll make it an order."

Feeling like a wet rag, Jake slumped against a bulkhead. "I'm glad that's over," he mumbled.

Sisko put his hand on Jake's shoulder. "Thank you,

son. But you had me worried sick. What in the world happened to you? Where did you go?"

"Dad," pleaded Jake, "I want to tell you the whole story. But first, may I go to bed? Please?"

"I think we've both had a long day," Sisko said. "Go straight to our quarters. I'll be along shortly."

Somehow or other Jake staggered all the way to his room without collapsing from sheer exhaustion. He fell into bed fully clothed, and he was asleep before he hit the mattress.

His father let him sleep until noon. Finally Sisko woke his son with a breakfast tray of toast, scrambled eggs, and orange juice. Jake munched away happily. After breakfast he took a quick shower and dressed in clean clothes. Then he joined his father in their living room. "What happened after I fell asleep?" he asked.

Sisko grinned at him. "You missed an exciting chase. Chok tried to outrun two Federation runabouts, but he couldn't. Then he threatened to open fire. That was a bluff. Chok hadn't been able to repair his shields, and firing without shields would have been suicide. In the end the Cardassians gave up."

"Dad, I don't understand. If Chok wanted to use Deep Space Nine for storage, why did he have his crew activate the bomb?"

Sisko gave him a grim smile. "Odo and I have talked about that. All that business about storing ores was a lie. You see, back when the Cardassians abandoned Deep Space Nine, Chok wanted to destroy it instead of turning it over to us. He set up the bomb, but for some reason he couldn't activate it. Odo's guess is that Starfleet arrived a little too soon for him."

Jake frowned. "So he made up the story about storing ores to come back and start the bomb. But why would he want to destroy the station now?" he asked.

Sisko replied, "Odo's theory is that Chok wanted to seize control of the Bajoran Wormhole. It's the most valuable resource in this quadrant, you know. First, Chok would blow up Deep Space Nine. Then he would call other Cardassian ships here—and by the time Starfleet could arrive, the Cardassians would have fortified their position. Since Chok failed, the Cardassian government would never admit to being involved in such an illegal plan, but Odo thinks they probably had some idea of what Chok was up to."

"What's going to happen to Chok and his crew?" asked Jake.

"A Federation trial," his father said firmly. "This morning I've been in touch with the Cardassian High Command. They claim Chok was a criminal, acting on his own."

"Do you believe that?"

Sisko shrugged. "It doesn't matter. The important thing is that since the Cardassians disown Chok's crew, there won't be an interstellar incident when the Federation tries them for terrorism."

Jake asked, "What happens if they're found guilty?"

"Well, the penalties for terrorism are strict," Sisko said. "They'd be sent to a rehabilitation facility—but since even the other Federation prisoners would hate the Cardassians, life would be chancy for them. I think it's more likely, though, that the Federation will turn them over to the Cardassians. You see, we believe the Cardassians still hold a number of Bajoran prisoners. If they really do, we can make some kind of prisoner swap. We'll give them their people back in exchange for the Bajorans."

"But, Dad—Chok tried to kill us," objected Jake. "It doesn't seem right that we should just hand him back."

Sisko's smile became grim. "Don't worry, Jake. Cardassians do not deal with their own kind lightly— especially if the prisoners have failed in an action against an enemy." He got up and stretched. "I've asked some friends to come to Ops a little later today. We all want to hear your whole story."

"I don't know whether you'll believe it or not," Jake told his father. "But I'll tell you everything that happened."

And in Ops a couple of hours later, Jake told quite an audience the whole amazing story of Dhraako and of the strange half existence he had led aboard Deep Space Nine. Keiko, Molly, O'Brien, Major Kira, Odo, Commander Sisko, Quark, and of course Nog listened to the whole tale. When she heard that Jake really had appeared to Molly, Keiko apologized for not believing her own daughter, but explained that she thought her husband had already spoken to Commander Sisko about Jake. She had assumed that the commander had found Jake safe and sound. Sisko wondered if there was any way of contacting Dhraako. "After all, we owe him our lives," he said.

"I don't think we can, Dad," Jake said. "He told me that Questers aren't supposed to reveal themselves. Now that someone knows Dhraako is here, he will have to leave."

Suddenly Molly spoke up: "Dhraako said to tell you he would leave at six—sixteen hundred," she said. "If you want to say good-bye."

Jake said, "Quick, Dad—what time is it?" They had a few minutes to spare. They all hurried to the large empty compartment that Dhraako had made headquarters ever since the building of Deep Space Nine. "Is he here?" asked Sisko.

"I don't see him," a disappointed Jake replied. "Nog?"

"No," the young Ferengi said. He had dressed in his best clothes, with a splendid emerald and gold head-band. "Molly, is Dhraako here?"

"Right there, silly," said Molly, pointing at thin air.

"Dad, have the lights lowered," Jake said.

"Computer, decrease illumination," Sisko ordered.

As the lights went down, Jake grinned. There was the tall, shimmering figure, barely visible. The red-orange eyes showed as two soft gleams. "I see him."

"So do I," said Nog. "Come to think of it, he doesn't look like a Ferengest at all."

"I wish I knew what you were talking about," grumbled Quark. "Idle chatter brings no profit, you know."

"I think I see," Odo said. "A kind of faint misti-ness."

Commander Sisko sighed. "I must be too old. He's

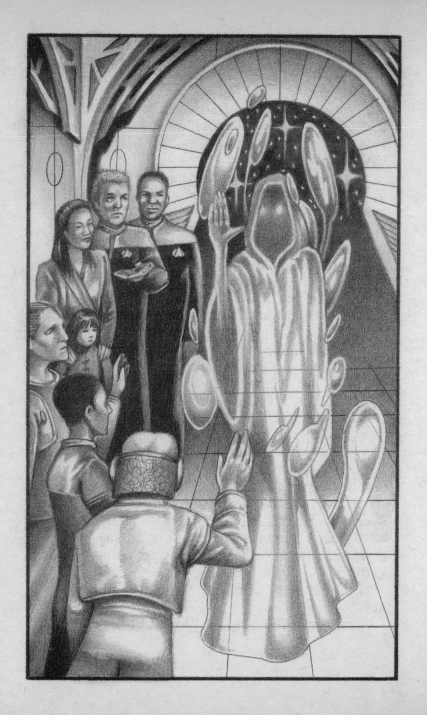

still invisible to me." He turned to Molly. "Molly, please tell Dhraako that all of us are grateful for his help. He is welcome on our station any time he wishes to return."

Molly said, "He knows that. Now he's saying good-bye."

Jake waved. So did Nog and Molly. With a grin Sisko did, too. After a moment even Odo, Kira, Keiko, O'Brien, and a very puzzled-looking Quark added their farewells.

"Oh," Molly said. "The table is opening up."

Jake turned his head and looked from the corners of his eyes. He could barely see the mushroom-shaped mechanism. It was unfolding, changing form. Now it encased the shape of Dhraako. It was so absurdly tiny—could it really be a starship?

"There he goes!" yelled Molly.

Jake blinked. He could not be sure, but he thought that the miniature ship had become a beam of energy and had zipped right through the wall.

O'Brien had taken out a portable scanner. "Slight energy flux," he said. "That's all."

"He's gone," Nog said.

With genuine regret Jake said, "Yeah. But I'll never forget him." He grinned at Nog. "You were really brave, do you know that? You thought I was a ghost, but you got over your fear and learned to communicate. That's really what saved us all."

"There's no profit in bravery," muttered Nog, looking pleased but embarrassed. "Anyway, you were the one who had to figure everything out. In the end you

117

and Dhraako saved us. I guess you protected us all. Jake Sisko, you were a real sheep!"

"Huh?" Jake asked.

"I'll have to explain that some other time," said Sisko, visibly fighting the urge to laugh.

Deep Space Nine rotated in space, once again peaceful and secure. From a view port Jake stared at the gleaming, endless stars of deep space. He knew that the Dhraakellian Quester was probably millions of miles away, an invisible streak of energy speeding through the Galaxy. Maybe, Jake thought, Dhraako would be a little less lonely with the memory of one friend to keep him company. He hoped so. After a few moments he turned away from the view port and grinned at Nog. "Now," said Jake, "what was that about *sheep?*"

About the Author

BRAD STRICKLAND has been writing science fiction and fantasy since 1982. He has published eight novels alone and two in collaboration with John Bellairs. In everyday life, Brad teaches English at Gainesville College and lives in Oakwood, Georgia, with his wife, Barbara, their son, Jonathan, their daughter, Amy, a huge white rabbit, one small dog, one large dog, six cats and an iguana. Although Brad is a big science fiction fan, he thinks that none of the inhabitants of his house are aliens, with the possible exception of two of the cats.

About the Illustrator

TODD CAMERON HAMILTON is a self-taught artist who has resided all his life in Chicago, Illinois. He has been a professional illustrator for the past ten years, specializing in fantasy, science fiction, and horror. His original works grace many private and corporate collections. He has co-authored two novels and several short stories. When not drawing, painting, or writing, his interests include metalsmithing, puppetry, and teaching.